TALES FROM THE CUBICLES

CHRONICLES OF CORPORATE COMEDY AND DRAMA

AF121030

MRIDULA PATHAK

NewDelhi • London

BLUEROSE PUBLISHERS
India | U.K.

Copyright © Mridula Pathak 2024

All rights reserved by author. No part of this publication may be reproduced, stored in a retrieval system or transmitted in any form or by any means, electronic, mechanical, photocopying, recording or otherwise, without the prior permission of the author. Although every precaution has been taken to verify the accuracy of the information contained herein, the publisher assume no responsibility for any errors or omissions. No liability is assumed for damages that may result from the use of information contained within.

BlueRose Publishers takes no responsibility for any damages, losses, or liabilities that may arise from the use or misuse of the information, products, or services provided in this publication.

For permissions requests or inquiries regarding this publication, please contact:

BLUEROSE PUBLISHERS
www.BlueRoseONE.com
info@bluerosepublishers.com
+91 8882 898 898
+4407342408967

ISBN: 978-93-5989-552-9

Cover design: Tahira
Typesetting: Tanya Raj Upadhyay

First Edition: February 2024

Dedication

To the valiant warriors of the corporate battlefield.

May this book serve as a beacon of inspiration during moments of fatigue and as a source of laughter in times of corporate craziness.

*"He who has a WHY
to live can bear almost any how."*

- Friedrich Nietzsche.

About the Author

Mridula grew up in a language-rich atmosphere, which helped her develop a deep awareness of the power and exquisite beauty that words carry. Her parents introduced her to the world of creativity and analysis, passing down the art of writing as a beloved family heirloom.

She succeeds in various fields and fulfils the roles of graphic designer, analyst, devoted mother, and loving wife. In addition to these responsibilities, she experiences great success in the realm of words. She considers writing the most effective communication method and a morally superior medium of expression.

Two guiding principles for her writing are straightforwardness and simplicity. She believes that simple, unembellished language can express the depth of feelings and thoughts. Each word is carefully chosen, and each sentence is written with the precision of a trained artisan. Her prose and poetry have a genuine quality that resonates with readers, resulting in a strong relationship and a deep connection.

When you read the words, she has looped with heart and soul, you will embark on a journey of introspection and discovery. The reader may find themselves unable to catch their breath as a result of her findings, which are presented through the elegance of language. Mridula's works have a sumptuous yet deeply realistic lyrical quality, and this is true whether she is analysing the complexities of human relationships or attempting to capture the fleeting beauty of nature.

Tales from the Cubicles is Mridula's second book. Her debut book, Maun Kolahal ki Anugunj is a collection of Hindi poetry.

Her poetry flawlessly blends emotion and language, reflecting their profundity. Her versatility allows her to reach a large audience and spread her themes of reflection, affection, and understanding across cultures.

Mridula uses various platforms to show readers the world from her unique perspective. Like a gentle breeze, her words can move the soul and leave an unforgettable mark on those who see her creation. Her writing has appeared in monthly and annual publications.

She can tell a captivating story about the human experience on stage or in writing. Her work inspires introspection, and her open-mic performances are unforgettable.

Mridula embodies the beauty of a purposeful life, whether creating stunning works of art, exploring life's complexity, navigating parenting, or penning elegant and honest words.

Disclaimer

Tales from the Cubicles is a work of fiction and serves as a personal journal, capturing the imaginative thoughts and expressions of the author. Any resemblance to real people, living or dead, or actual events is purely coincidental. The purpose of this work is not to harm, injure, or offend anyone.

The author affirms that no malicious intent or harm was intended in creating this work. The purpose is solely to explore the realms of imagination and share personal reflections through the medium of written expression. Readers are encouraged to approach the content with the understanding that it is a fictional narrative and that any perceived similarities to real-life events or individuals are coincidental.

डॉ. रमेश पोखरियाल 'निशंक'
Dr. Ramesh Pokhriyal 'Nishank'
सांसद, हरिद्वार (लोकसभा)
पूर्व शिक्षा मंत्री, भारत सरकार
पूर्व मुख्यमंत्री, उत्तराखण्ड

Member of Parliament, Haridwar (Lok Sabha)
Former Education Minister, Govt. of India
Former Chief Minister, Uttarakhand

20, तुगलक क्रिसेंट, नई दिल्ली-110011
20, Tughlak Crescent, New Delhi-110011
दूरभाष : 011-21430588
Phone : 011-21430588

Email : drrameshpokhriyal@gmail.com
: drrameshpokhriyal@sansad.nic.in

Well Wishes

Dear Mridula Pathak Jee,

I received a copy of your book "TALES FROM THE CUBICLES". Words penned in the book are truly reflecting the expressions of the modern offices often acts as a living society in itself. Tales from the cubicles celebrate ordinary theatricals in which deadlines become narrative points and coffee breaks serve as intermissions. As one travel through the corridors of cubicles, may find humor in the ordinary, solace in the shared challenges and perhaps a hint of nostalgia for corporate adventures.

The book very well represents the most of the offices of new socio-economic system that are on the way to explore the characters making dynamicity at the work place.

I hope my wishes will encourage you to continue your writing on different aspects and emotions of life for greater humanity.

DR. RAMESH POKHRIYAL 'NISHANK'

स्थायी निवास : 37/1 रवीन्द्र नाथ टैगोर मार्ग, विजय कॉलोनी, देहरादून, उत्तराखण्ड-248001
दूरभाष : 0135-2718899
Permanent Address : 37/1, Ravindra Nath Tagore Marg, Vijay Colony, Dehradun, Uttarakhand-248001
Telephone : 0135-2718899

Acknowledgement

The evolution of "Tales from the Cubicles" has been a voyage of much joy and mirth, flakes of frustration, mutual camaraderie and great collaboration in the corporate trenches.

It is far simpler to write a book than it is to write an acknowledgement, because I frequently find myself at a loss for words, and words seem powerless to express my gratitude to people who have supported me throughout my life, without whom I would not be who I am or what I do.

Thank you, Maa and Papa. Without your unconditional support and love, this book never would have come to be.

My heartfelt gratitude to my husband, who inspires me every day with his incredible thoughtfulness, whose insistence transformed my scattered musings into the tapestry of narratives you now hold. His gentle nudges and, dare I say it, deadline-setting skills moved me through the maze of procrastination and into the domain of authorship.

Thank you to friends and family, the genuine architects of inspiration, for kindly sharing their stories from the corporate mining tales. Your experiences, grievances, and triumphant moments have been woven into this book's fabric, transforming it into a collective tale that speaks to each corporate professional.

A particular thanks to those who believed in this endeavour and provided motivation and support through words, caffeine-infused chats, and the occasional virtual pat on the back. Your belief in the stories presented in these pages has been the wind beneath my cubicle wings.

Thanks to all those who took the time out of their extremely hectic schedules to read an advance copy of this book and write endorsements: Gaurav Srivastava, Rahul Borooah, Saurav Singh, Rahul Mishra, Vineet Gupta, Sambhu, Sudhir, Vishnu, Abhishek.

And to the readers who are now embarking on this voyage through the frequently amusing, occasionally frustrating, but unquestionably sympathetic stories, your presence is the finishing flourish in this corporate symphony.

May the giggles be plentiful, the coffee always perfect (the way you like it, hot or cold, frothy or expresso), and the stories from the cubicles echo through the halls of your own professional adventures.

With honest gratitude and a virtual high-five.

Preface

In life's ever-changing fabric and plot, there is a peculiar environment hidden behind the towering glass facades and polished veneer of professionalism: the corporate jungle. As I write these stories from my cubicle (modernise the cubicle with the low partition office layout, adding a little description for you to picture), chuckling in the midst of imminent deadlines, I welcome you, my dear reader, to join me on a journey across the bizarre environment where neckties serve as camouflage, coffee-stained tables as war zones, and heaps of documents and reports unroll as scrolls of wisdom.

This narrative is a tribute to an untamed province where white-collar warriors wander and the everyday struggle becomes a big adventure. These pages contain narratives that traverse cubicle-filled landscapes, unravel the enigmatic language of the water cooler, Maggie Point, and smoke zone conversations, and expose the hidden lessons lingering in the air, saturated with the aroma of coffee, smoke, and some fumes here and there (not literally though, but where there is fire, the remnants will linger in the form of fumes and ashes).

The choice of neckties and footwear in this setting is more than just a sartorial statement; it is a visual code that hints at the layers beneath the crisply ironed shirts and immaculate blouses. As we progress through the chapters, deciphering the symbolism of neckwear and footwear, we discover the complexities of a world where looks can deceive and actual character is buried beneath the mask of professionalism.

The mound of reports, like old scrolls, records the battles waged and won, the victories that were celebrated, and the losses grieved. These reports are more than just artefacts; they are concrete evidence of corporate drama, with each blot and smudge telling a story about the battles of the daily grind.

The cubicle-filled landscapes meticulously described in these pages are more than just physical spaces, ergonomic furniture, or immaculately designed interiors with a restrained material and colour palette to make them feel larger while reflecting a relaxing vibe; they are theatres of absurdity, where the mundane transforms into the extraordinary. The drama unfolds in this microcosm of the workplace, where every cubicle is a kingdom and each employee is a distinct species—a story of survival, camaraderie, and, at times, an outright chuckle with unsuppressed mirth.

As we decipher the business jargon and the whispers from the breakout area, we reach the social nexus, where alliances are formed, rumours spread like a gentle breeze from the smoke corner, and strategic manoeuvres take place under cover of casual talks. The water cooler and beverage dispenser, which are frequently dismissed as ordinary hydration stations, become a focal point where the pulse of the office is sensed and the dynamics of the corporate ecology are discreetly managed.

Amidst the bustle and unpredictability, there is a perfect opportunity to find the humour that lurks in the most unexpected places, the friendship that blooms amid deadlines and meetings, and the essential life lessons that permeate the coffee-scented air.

Fasten your seatbelts as we begin this crazy and often wild journey into the corporate jungle. Within the turmoil is a narrative worth telling—one of tenacity, personal growth, and profound beauty concealed beyond the surface of daily routines. Welcome to "Tales from the Cubicles," where the corporate wilderness is not simply a backdrop but an integral part of the stories that unfold within.

Through the revolving door and turnstile, you'll be plunged into a bustling environment teeming with a broad array of employees, each dressed in business casual attire and equipped with their own individual quirks and oddities. It's a place where deadlines loom like storm clouds and the workplace printer is handled with the veneration of an ancient artefact.

Now, let us put on our imagined pith helmets and start on a satirical safari through the dangerous terrain of the corporate world and culture. It is true that a touch of humour goes a long way toward winning over the crowd.

Table of Contents

Chapter 1: Lost in the Corporate Wilderness 1

Chapter 2: The Species of the Office Savannah 8

Chapter 3: Where Cubicles Collide and Characters Converge 12

Chapter 4: The Procrastination Prodigy Chronicle in the Corporate Circus 18

Chapter 5: The Marvelous Menagerie of Corporate Commanders 23

Chapter 6: The Emoji Enthusiast (EE): A Symphony of Symbols 33

Chapter 7: The Secret Office Romance 37

Chapter 8: The Coffee Cappers 42

Chapter 9: The Trials and the Tribulations 46

Chapter 10: The Acronym Avalanche 51

Chapter 11: Conjunctivitis Survivor 58

Chapter 12: Gossip Mongers: The Unsung Heroes of Corporate Hilarity 64

Chapter 13: Job Interviews: The Theatrical Spectacle of Corporate Courtship 68

Chapter 14: The Multitasking Marvel: Juggling Genius or Overworked Superhero? 73

Chapter 15: Office Meetings: The Black Hole of Productivity 79

Chapter 16: The Whimsical World of MT: Mandatory Training 84

Chapter 17: From Pipeline to Potluck: The Triumph of Team Feast 89

Chapter 18: The Quagmire of Workplace Credit Hoga 94

Chapter 19: Perks and Quirks: Unveiling the Enigma .. 99

Chapter 20: Promotion and Politics 104

Reviews 110

Chapter 1:
Lost in the Corporate Wilderness

I was born and raised in a milieu that was far away from the corporate sphere. When both of your parents work in the government sector and you are married to an Olive Green, established conventions—the rule books—dominantly govern your behaviour in a place where traditions, customs, beliefs, and habits passed down from one generation to the next have consistently maintained a high degree of civility.

As a result of my husband's occupation, I have thus far led a peripatetic life, an experience I have greatly cherished. With the intention of establishing ourselves, beginning a modest degree of stability, and relocating to a competent dwelling in a major metropolitan area, I made the decision to challenge myself by embracing the change and joining a larger and more reputable brand while ensuring that my work-life balance remains unaffected. Should I have mentioned the stability that a consistent pay check provides?

Due to my ill health, I decided to take a sabbatical—a break from the hustle and bustle of my full-time job—in the middle of my corporate journey. It was not an idyllic moment per se. The pause from the professional world helped me to rethink and redefine the conception of productivity. It wasn't about perpetual mobility but rather a deliberate balance, a regulated tempo that matched the rhythm of my health. The break became a canvas for self-discovery, a period of transformation from which I emerged not just physically refreshed but also with a revitalized sense of purpose and creativity.

During my sabbatical, I discovered a blossoming garden of creativity within myself.

The corporate environment cordially welcomes individuals, extending assurances of career advancement, financial security, and professional satisfaction. Unbeknownst to you at the moment, the entrance is a meticulously constructed illusion—a mirage—which obscures the complex tunnel of mazes that you are about to traverse.

The maze becomes increasingly restrictive as one progresses through this Maze 9 to 5. Meetings, deadlines, and communications proliferate throughout the day, with each interruption seemingly resulting in nothing.

The 9-to-5 workday becomes an interminable cycle in which the boundaries between professional and personal life become indistinct.

Ah! I discovered that the concrete and steel wilderness that is the corporate world had consumed me in its entirety. When I first entered the building, the lobby was filled with sterilized air conditioning, and the sound of heels clicking set the tone for my new existence. I was oblivious to the fact that beneath the veneer of professionalism lay an uncharted wilderness comprised of business suits, neckties, and meetings that would hardly accomplish the desired outcome.

Long shadows were cast by the morning sun across the open office, which was adorned with rows of cubicles that stood silently as sentinels of war. Every cubicle represented a kingdom, and each employee represented a distinct species contending with the daily challenge of survival. The murmur of the coffee machines' comforting background music stood in stark contrast to the unpredictable behaviour of my recently met colleagues.

Acquiring my cubicle marked the initial step of my expedition into this corporate wilderness. From navigating the labyrinthine layout to deciphering the unspoken regulations of territorial rights, the quest was fraught with obstacles. As I acclimatized to my ergonomic throne, enveloped by glass walls and white-grey partitions, I couldn't help but be transported to a dystopian realm, where the cubicle simultaneously functioned as a fortress and prison.

The reports, which resembled ancient manuscripts in that they were stained with fingerprints and highlighted in colour, detailed the successes and failures of the corporate tribe. With every spill, an indelible impression is made on time, symbolising the strenuous nature of office warfare. The esteemed sanctuary's breakroom stocked coffee, the invigorating elixir of life that energized the corporate realm's routine as well as diplomatic endeavours.

Board meetings were rendered less strategic than the enigmatic corner conversations that transpired in this peculiar world. Alliances were formed, and rumours meandered like a meandering river behind the communal refrigerator, which served as a social focus. I acquired the intricate art of casual conversation during my time here, where the ability to carry on small talk was crucial for survival and uttering the incorrect word could result in social exile.

As I silently scrutinised my fellow workers, I was astounded by the variety of species that inhabited the corporate savannah. Conspicuously aware of the most recent rumours, the Office Gossiper prowled the corridors, skilfully amassing and distributing information in a feline fashion. Equipped with a weaponized mouse and a time-freezing glare, the Keyboard Warrior fought covert skirmishes on the digital frontlines.

Within this heterogeneous ecosystem, I came across the enigmatic Email Ninja, an expert in clandestine correspondence. They adeptly traversed the perilous landscape of the inbox, transmitting messages with the lightning-fast speed of an enigmatic emissary. Their ability was legendary, and while their presence was frequently felt, it was rarely observed.

As the days progressed into weeks and the weeks into months, I came to the realization that the corporate jungle was a theatre of craziness and not merely a place of survival. At that moment, the ordinary was elevated to the extraordinary, and the extraordinary was transformed into the magnificently extraordinary. The pantry discussions were not mere rumours; rather, they were covert strategic alliances being formed. Board meetings transcended mere deliberations, transforming into meticulously planned spectacles in which every member contributed to the overarching structure of corporate culture.

My expedition through this peculiar realm evolved into an individual odyssey. I mastered the art of gamifying the quotidian, deciphered the unfathomable language of buzzwords, and manoeuvred through the complexities of office politics. The colour-coded reports served as a navigational tool, providing direction through the unfamiliar landscape of interdepartmental dynamics.

Amidst the perilous corporate landscape, I encountered unforeseen allies and confronted formidable adversaries. The fluorescent lights ascended above the office political battlefield and emanated a surreal glow reminiscent of distant stars. I acquired knowledge of the art of survival during my time here, which involved a nuanced interplay of diplomacy, wit, and humour.

With the progression of the days into nights and the subsequent recovery from corporate conquests over the weekends, I developed a deeper admiration for the aesthetic value concealed amidst the disorder. The corporate jungle, in all its peculiarities and idiosyncrasies, served as a platform for both personal and professional development. It was a location where individuals developed resilience, interpersonal connections were challenged, and unexpected insights into life's lessons were gained.

Months later, while still intact and entangled in this labyrinth, the prospect of an exit appears to beckon from every nook and cranny of the corporate wilderness. Amid the distance, signs that read "Work-Life Balance," "Promotion," and "Career Advancement" shimmered like mirages. However, as you draw closer, they dissipate, leaving you bewildered and unsure of the feasibility of your escape.

The expedition is not devoid of obstacles and peculiarities. A location that one visits on a daily basis, aspiring to catch a glimpse of the exit while finding comfort in the companionship of other nomadic individuals. Despite the apparent difficulty of escaping, the corporate travellers can benefit significantly from the fortitude and flexibility developed in this wilderness.

Therefore, as you traverse the maze's turns and obstacles, bear in mind the fact that while it is possible to exit at any moment, liberating oneself from the clutches of corporate entrapment necessitates considerably more than a combination of audacity, ingenuity, and a dash of wit to illuminate the way.

Chapter 2:
The Species of the Office Savannah

Greetings, dear readers and folks from the concrete wild space, an environment imbued with the distinct aroma of freshly brewed coffee and where the resounding chirp of the office printer fills the space. Adaptability, wit, and a dependable caffeine source are critical factors in determining day-to-day survival in the uncharted wilderness, characterized by colour-coded reports and neckties.

Upon entering this corporate ecosystem, one will come across a multitude of species, each possessing unique characteristics and strategies for survival. For instance, the elusive Office Gossiper constructs a complex network of intrigue that rivals any political drama by feeding on the most recent murmurs and innuendos. Carefully observe as they stealthily traverse the corridors of the office, engaging in deep glances and subdued murmurs that elevate discussions to covert operations.

The majestic Keyboard Warrior, on the other hand, is in charge of the digital savannah and has a vast collection of emails as well as a remarkable talent for writing passive-aggressive messages. Pay attention as their dexterous fingertips traverse the keyboard, producing an endless stream of scrupulously crafted messages that have the potential to intimidate even the most experienced peer. It is a sight to behold how easily the Keyboard Warrior displays dominance from the convenience of their ergonomic chair.

Keep a watch out for the perilous Email Ninja as you circumnavigate the cubicle-filled environment—an exclusively designed space with comfortable ergonomic furniture and lounge seating is used to create casual collaboration and meeting areas. These elusive beings, adept at deception and covert manoeuvrability, convey communications with a level of accuracy comparable to that of a ninja. They navigate the digital fringe in silence. Their influence is felt in the inbox shadows; however, if you blink, you may fail to notice their existence.

However, the corporate jungle is a complex ecosystem in which collaboration and cooperation are critical for survival; it is not merely a habitat for workers. Introducing the Conference Room Diplomat, an elite species that proficiently manoeuvres through the perilous universe of group dynamics. Observe as they deftly organize meetings, guiding individuals with differing perspectives toward a common objective, or as far as a vague action item goes.

In the interim, the Intern Voyager, an iterative species in pursuit of expertise and understanding, navigates the cubicle canyons with open eyes and a strong desire to assimilate the undisclosed realities of the corporate labyrinth. Do they have the ability to acclimate to the office's rituals and customs, or do they succumb to the challenges and difficulties that arise from coffee-fetching missions and blunders with photocopiers?

Observe the mating rituals that transpire in the dimly illuminated corners of the break room during lunch as the day progresses in this dynamic ecosystem. Proficient individuals among colleagues partake in a nuanced exchange of information in the course of informal dialogue, thereby forging connections with the intention of upholding an image of professionalism.

The observation of spontaneous alliances emerging over matters such as weekend plans, mutual disgust towards the malfunctioning office elevator, and annoying managers underscores the strategic significance of beverage dispenser conversations. The participants assume the roles of kings and pawns, representing the most recent Netflix series and the keys to office supply storage, respectively, in this social chess game.

Within the boundaries of the workplace, mere task completion and meeting deadlines are insufficient for survival; one must also discern the intricate nuances of workplace dynamics. The corporate jungle serves as a platform for the theatrical transformation of the ordinary, with each employee contributing to this elaborate spectacle.

Please secure your seatbelt and prepare to embark on a more profound exploration of the complexities inherent in the corporate circus. Observe, enjoy, and celebrate the various species that populate the office savannah.

As you engage in this satirical expedition, you will discover that each report and coffee-stained desk conceal a narrative and that each conversation signifies the progression of a strategic dance. The page-turning journey in "Tales from Cubicles" commences as the untamed aspects of corporate culture are exposed.

Chapter 3:
Where Cubicles Collide and Characters Converge

"If life throws you lemons, make lemonade" is a traditional adage that encourages a positive and proactive approach to dealing with challenges or disappointments, and I wholeheartedly support this mentality. Not only am I making the best of undesirable circumstances by turning them into lemonade, but I'm also generously sharing the fruits of my perseverance with you, dear readers.

So, returning to our unfinished business of deciphering the cryptic corporate, where fluorescent lights flicker like dim stars, keyboard clicks clack, and printer hums form an ambient soundtrack, and a goal is much more than an inspiration but a dream with a deadline, I found myself immersed in the daily drama of the workplace.

As the clock struck one and people raced through their cubicles, it became clear that this seemingly mundane workspace was anything but ordinary—it was a stage. I, along with my colleagues, were the eccentric actors, each contributing to the incredible spectacle of office life.

The first act took place in the cubicles, where the sound of keyboard clicks and the occasional phone ring set the tone for our shared existence. I met Monica, the queen of color-coded spreadsheets and a papyrophiliac; her love of elegant stationery was well-known—perhaps it was more than just love—an obsession may be; she also defended her area with the devotion of a dragon protecting its treasure. Monica's cubicle was a colourful mosaic of Post-it notes, each having a cryptic meaning that only she understood.

Then there's Bonnie, a little fellow and the office philosopher who steals (read almost ruins) the show by turning regular coffee breaks into not-so-deep talks about the meaning of life, frequently leaving us contemplating our existence while sipping piping hot turned lukewarm beverages. His cubicle (read: mind and soul), loaded with inspirational posters and a little zen garden, served as the unofficial headquarters for existential pondering. Dare you to say anything; he will shower you with two thousand words of wisdom that only he comprehends. Mr. Bonnie, a bachelor not sure by choice or by force, had something more than encryption and was most likely suffering from the incurable I Am the Best syndrome.

As I explored the mysterious conference rooms 10.3 and 10.4, the pantry, the lounge, and the breakout area, I met a whole new set of personalities. Mrs. Smitha, the scary figure of the no-nonsense colleague, wielded the procedure as if she were casting a spell. In her presence, deadlines were religious ceremonies, and tardiness was considered heresy.

Sara, Kiran, and Deep, the irreverent trio, turned each meeting into a comic show with their quick wit and hilarious remarks. Their shenanigans in the conference room provided a pleasant break from the routine of PowerPoint presentations and monthly business reports.

Kiran, an experienced and tenured team member, is an undisputed specialist in navigating the complex web of dos and don'ts. Her ability to conjure excuses at the last minute is nothing short of an art, and no one could ever challenge or question the immaculately crafted excuses. You would be wondering why I highlight Kiran; for a simple reason, I need to steal this particular skill from her arsenal.

Regardless of how meticulously I plan and rehearse for the big show, I always seem to stumble and fumble at the last minute. Take a bow, dear Kiran, for an outstanding performance, which is often strategically timed just before the weekend. The trail of envy she leaves behind among her colleagues demonstrates the utter creativity of her excuse-crafting abilities; she has elevated the art of excuse-making to unprecedented heights. Her ability to elegantly navigate unexpected obstacles is something many people aspire to, transforming the mundane act of making excuses into a captivating performance that makes colleagues green with envy.

While navigating the ancient caffeine-consuming procedure, the Coffee Kung Fu Master and the disciples performs sophisticated martial arts techniques to create that perfect cup. They walk through the office kitchen holding a thermos that appears to defy gravity, elevating the prosaic task of making coffee into an art form. The Coffee Kung Fu Master's knowledge of caffeine science earns them respect among colleagues seeking the elixir of life.

Meanwhile, the Email Escapologist exhibits their ability to write emails that are both lengthy and opaque. Their texts contain needless details, convoluted words, and a host of abbreviations that only they understand. Colleagues who get emails from the Email Escapologist embark on a deciphering expedition to uncover the secret meanings contained within the electronic message. The best part is the flawless use of emoticons, which only Google can recognize and comprehend.

It's easy to miss the Elevator Eavesdropper, a silent observer in the vertical transportation chamber; the couple hone their skills at quietly overhearing portions of conversations. The partners in crime take strategic places in the elevator, taking up the gossip, rumours, and office drama that travels in whispers.

The Elevator Eavesdropper becomes an accidental confidant in the office's common ideas, changing the elevator into a hidden hub of information sharing. If a certain piece of information needs to be widely conveyed, the best location is right next to the coffee vending machine.

As time passed, it became apparent that the workplace was a realm of insanity, where ordinary responsibilities were compared to glorious exploits, and elevator conversations were elevated to the seriousness of Shakespearean dialogues. Every colleague contributed to the workplace environment with their unique aesthetic, transforming it into a kaleidoscope of eccentricities and distinct personalities.

However, beneath the surface of this amusing comedy lies an unexpected truth: each character's unwavering will to create a cocoon of work and accomplishments. Behind the various characters and unusual deeds was a unifying goal: to effectively navigate the jungle of systems and deadlines in pursuit of professional achievement.

I couldn't help but admire the stunning reality of office life as I observed this unique combination of theatrics and concentration. The cubicles and conference rooms were more than just places to work; they served as the backdrop for the productivity masterpiece, a theatre where characters of all kinds collaborated to create a one-of-a-kind and unforgettable spectacle. So, with a better appreciation of the absurdity of it all, I anxiously await the next episode of "The Office Chronicles."

At the same time, while everyone else was preoccupied with their separate tasks, I was able to carve out time from my demanding schedule to diligently document the daily events happening on the tenth floor, which provided an excellent panoramic view from both inside and outside. I intended to portray this with eloquence through my use of language, carefully selecting each word to the best of my ability.

Chapter 4:
The Procrastination Prodigy:
Chronicle in the Corporate Circus

Embracing procrastination as an art form might seem counterintuitive in the world of productivity, but there's a certain charm to mastering the delicate dance between deadlines, productivity, and a tinge of creativity as well. On many occasions, I find myself yearning to attain the status of the Maestro of Procrastination. As I divulge some light-hearted advice (which I learned recently, but not yet mastered) to assist you in manoeuvring through this peculiar art form, we welcome you to meet the enigmatic individual we adoringly label "The Procrastination Prodigy" (PP) within the vibrant environment of this multi-story corporate headquarters in the urban core.

The PP, distinguished by the formidable fortification of discarded coffee cups that encircles his work area, is the unequivocal master of giving the impression of activity while actually accomplishing nothing substantial. One is essentially observing a magician at work with the cups proliferating throughout the day, which upholds the illusion of productivity.

In their natural habitat, the PP is often found navigating the wild terrains of social media sites with the agility of a digital ninja. Scrolling through feeds, liking memes and the latest trending hashtags, and scrolling through the Ecommerce sites—all in the name of "research," of course. Their exceptional proficiency in technology renders them the current rulers of the virtual procrastination monarchy.

They boast an awe-inspiring collection of "urgent" tasks, each adorned with the prestigious label of impending doom. These tasks, however, have mastered the art of postponement, creating an illusionary sense of urgency that lingers indefinitely. It's as if time itself bows down to the PP's procrastinative prowess.

If you ever aspire to emulate PP's prowess in fabricating fictitious justifications, such as attributing the recent malfunction of your fictitious time-traveling device or attributing the lack of progress on a given task to the alignment of the planets, allow your imagination to run wild when providing such explanations.

Concurrently, it would be necessary to orchestrate a symphony of diversions that serve to shift focus from outstanding obligations. Motivate the postponement with grandiose diversions, such as an unexpected fascination with secret anecdotes or an imperative requirement to rearrange one's workspace.

What sets the PP apart is their ability to avoid the ever-watchful gaze of higher-ups. With a cloak of invisibility woven from the threads of delayed deadlines, strategically planned breaks for solace, and, of course, well-deserved meal breaks (which are impossible to deny or postpone), they have perfected this ability to the point where their superiors are blissfully oblivious that the PP's workstation is a productivity black hole.

Consider the scenario where a manager glances at the PP's computer screen, which is adorned with a complex arrangement of graphs and charts, ignorant of the fact that it is a sophisticated spreadsheet containing fantasy football scores that has been deceitfully posed as project analytics. The manner in which the PP skilfully merges the ordinary and the fantastical is truly praiseworthy.

Another noteworthy occurrence transpired amidst the disorder, presenting the Procrastination Prodigy's abilities in an especially comical manner. A critical project deadline was rapidly approaching, and the team was diligently striving to complete the tasks before the cutoff. Meetings were held, strategies were devised, and everyone was putting their best foot forward—except for our exceptionally talented Procrastination Prodigy. Because PP was found running and hoping the bays seeking help from other colleagues who were not part of the project and efficiently delegating the tasks at the last minute, what caught the attention of the entire office, including usually stern-faced managers, found themselves caught up in the hilarity of the moment.

When queried about their apparent neglect of the approaching deadline, the Procrastination Prodigy responded with a sigh and explained that they operate most effectively when time is of the essence. Unbeknownst to all, the Procrastination Prodigy underwent an unexpected metamorphosis at midnight on the final day of the deadline, blossoming into a work prodigy who delivered a flawless project that filled the entire team with admiration.

Although their tendency to procrastinate may cause confusion among their peers and may also leave colleagues shaking their heads in frustration, their adeptness at managing the intricate balance between time constraints and innovative thinking is indeed endearing. In the broader picture, the Procrastination Prodigy exemplifies the intricate equilibrium required to maintain the thriving side hustle of online window browsing while appearing diligent.

Therefore, the next time you observe a desk laden with coffee cups and a seemingly occupied person engrossed in social media, you may have encountered the Procrastination Prodigy, an unsung hero of procrastination in the corporate circus who possesses a unique combination of qualities and a propensity for postponing the inevitable.

Chapter 5:
The Marvellous Menagerie of Corporate Commanders

In the hallowed halls of the corporate kingdom, where the scent of ambition and the aroma of freshly brewed coffee intertwine, one cannot help but marvel at the diverse array of managerial species that roam the cubicle-clad savannah.

Join me, dear reader, on an illuminating expedition into the enchanting world of corporate management, where the leaders are as varied and peculiar as the flora and fauna of our country.

It's been 2 years and a few months in my current organization, and I'm continuing to stand tall. Ratings, appraisals, and recognition are all in place, with no challenges as such. In short, so far, so good (that's what I once said (and continue to do so) when asked if I was facing any challenges or issues that needed to be addressed during my probation period). Throughout my service to this organization, and up to this date, I have remained steadfast in my commitment to it.

I've served with eight high-flying commanders (only time will tell who will fly to what height). They have all been so diverse in their ways. While I fleetingly elaborate on all my experiences and understandings, I will refrain from taking names and the sequence of their tenures. But one thing which I need to mention explicitly is one of my managers, who was an amalgamation of all the undermentioned traits, and he also happens to be my favourite. Others have characteristics that set them apart from the crowd. So, dear readers, strap on your humour hats and brace yourselves for the satirical journey ahead.

The Micromanaging Maestro: A Symphony of Obsession

Ah, the Micromanaging Maestro, a species so rare and elusive that encountering one is akin to spotting a unicorn at the water dispenser. I had the distinct pleasure of working under the watchful eye of Maestro Max, a virtuoso of vexation. Armed with a magnifying glass and a penchant for perfection, Max had an unparalleled ability to scrutinise the minute details of any project.

My first encounter with the Maestro occurred when I innocently attempted to format a routine report. Little did I know that my font size, paragraph spacing, and use of words would become the subject of a forensic investigation. It was as if I had committed a heinous crime against the sacred art of document formatting.

"I don't want to see a single pixel out of place!" exclaimed Maestro Max, his eyes ablaze with the fervor of a thousand proof-readers.

Every task, no matter how inconsequential, fell under the watchful gaze of the Maestro. It was not uncommon to receive emails with subject lines like "Urgent: Font Size Emergency" or "Critical: Commas in Disarray." One could almost hear the distant echo of a classical symphony playing as the Maestro conducted his meticulous inspections.

To survive in the Maestro's kingdom, one must develop ninja-like agility in dodging the scrutinising gaze. Quick formatting skills, a well-honed ability to foresee potential pixel outages, and a dash of humility were essential tools in navigating the treacherous landscape of micromanagement.

The Inspirational Oracle: Where Motivation Meets Confusion

In the heart of every corporate hierarchy lies the den of the Inspirational Oracle, a mythical being whose motivational prowess rivals that of a self-help guru on steroids. My journey into the zen zone of the Inspirational Oracle began with a mandatory team-building seminar that promised to unlock the hidden potential within each team member.

To truly understand what my colleagues and I are going through, esteemed readers you must envision this: a dimly lit conference room adorned with motivational captions, a screen displaying a serene mountain landscape (the typical Windows screen saver, just to save you the extra effort of imagination), and the faint scent of lavender wafting through the air (Air Wick freshmatic room freshener-the admin's generosity bestowed upon us). Enter Oracle Ojas, a vision in flowing robes and a headset microphone, ready to unleash a torrent of inspiration on the unsuspecting crowd.

"Team, we are not just colleagues; we are a family on a quest for greatness!" declared Oracle Ojas, his voice echoing through the room like a mystical incantation.

With every passing PowerPoint slide, Ojas delved into the depths of his reservoir of inspirational quotes. From Confucius to Oprah, no sage or talk show host was spared in his quest to uplift our spirits. The team, however, found themselves grappling with the profound question: Were we here to achieve corporate glory or embark on a spiritual awakening?

As the Oracle continued his motivational monologue, brimming with heartfelt anecdotes and a sprinkle of tears, the team sat in bewildered silence for not less than an hour, wondering about the SLAs they were on the verge of missing and fretting about the OTs on the weekends. Were we truly on the brink of a collective epiphany, or were we unwitting participants in an avant-garde theatre production?

Navigating the terrain of the Inspirational Oracle required mastering the art of nodding in agreement with no offensive expressions, facial or otherwise, while internally pondering the relevance of aligning our chakras in the pursuit of quarterly targets.

The Invisible Phantom: A Ghostly Mirage of Management

In the intricate maze of corporate complexities, a mysterious figure silently weaves through the shadows—the elusive Invisible Phantom. Unseen yet ever-present, this enigmatic entity navigates the corridors of power, leaving behind a trail of intrigue and speculation.

A spectral manager whose presence is as elusive as the company's Wi-Fi during a crucial video conference. I had the honour (or was it a curse?) of reporting to Phantom Phil, a manager so adept at invisibility that even Houdini would be envious.

Communication with the Phantom Phil was an art form in and of itself. Emails from the elusive manager were cryptic missives filled with vague instructions and mysterious acronyms. It was not uncommon to receive messages like, "FYI: EOD update required ASAP. TIA," leaving the recipient in a state of confusion reminiscent of deciphering ancient hieroglyphics.

Team meetings, if they occurred at all, were conducted via teleconferencing software, where Phantom Phil's pixelated avatar resembled a spectral figure communicating from ethereal territory. The team members' questions were answered ambiguously, leading to more questions than answers.

"Phil, do you think we should proceed with Plan A or consider Plan B?" I once dared to ask during a virtual huddle.

The reply was mysterious and consisted of a brief pause and the phrase "Let's circle back on that offline. Thanks."

At that very moment, I knew the repercussions and the feedback that I would receive offline for my heinous crime.

To navigate the territory of the Invisible Phantom, one had to develop a sixth sense for deciphering coded messages and interpreting the subtle nuances of virtual body language. It was a skill set that bordered on clairvoyance, for only those attuned to the whispers of the corporate winds could hope to unravel the secrets of the Invisible Phantom.

The Spreadsheet Sorcerer: Conjuring Chaos in Columns and Rows

Behold the Spreadsheet Sorcerer, a manager whose domain is the incomprehensible Microsoft Excel. I found myself under the spell of Sorcerer Sam, a master of arcane formulas and pivot table incantations. To this day, I shudder at the memory of Sam's scrutinizing gaze as he reviewed my expense reports with the precision of an accountant on a caffeine bender.

The Sorcerer's lair was adorned with charts and graphs that seemed to dance to an otherworldly rhythm. Pivot tables floated in mid-air, and conditional formatting spells brought colour to a grayscale world of numbers. Sam revelled in the art of data manipulation, turning mundane project updates into visually stunning masterpieces.

"Behold the power of the VLOOKUP!" Sam would exclaim, as if summoning a benevolent deity from the depths of spreadsheet oblivion.

To survive in the land of the Spreadsheet Sorcerer, one had to become an apprentice in the dark arts of data manipulation. Proficiency in Excel became a rite of passage, and the ability to conjure meaningful insights from the abyss of raw data was a skill worthy of admiration.

Yet, amid the enchanting glow of pivot tables and the hypnotic dance of pie charts, one couldn't shake the feeling that, perhaps, the Spreadsheet Sorcerer had lost touch with reality beyond the borders of the spreadsheet kingdom.

Emergency Enthusiast: Beacon of Chaos

In the grand tapestry of managerial diversity, the Emergency Enthusiast stands as a beacon of chaos. The emergency enthusiast is a marvel to behold in the never-ending workplace circus. With their flair for the dramatic, unmatched knack for overreaction, and relentless ability to turn the mundane into the extraordinary, they keep their colleagues on the edge of their swivel chairs, waiting for the next act in this never-ending drama of epic proportions. So, brace yourselves, dear office dwellers, for you know him, but you never know when a routine paper cut might lead to the most dramatic email chain of your professional lives.

The Crisis Connoisseur: Turning Molehills into Volcanoes

My encounter with Crisis Connoisseur Mini was a rollercoaster of adrenaline-fueled drama that left the team questioning the very definition of urgency.

It all began with a seemingly innocent email subject: "URGENT: Coffee Machine Malfunction!" In a flurry of panic-inducing messages, Mini declared a state of emergency, summoning IT specialists and maintenance crews to address the dire situation at the beverage station. The machine is out of order. While others grumble, the Crisis Connoisseur sees this as an opportunity for a full-blown coffee crisis and declares it a "caffeine catastrophe," ensuring everyone feels the weight of the situation.

"Team, this is Code Red! We cannot function without our caffeine fix. I repeat, Code Red!" exclaimed Mini, her urgency eclipsing the severity of the actual.

The Crisis Connoisseur thrives on turning mundane mishaps into epic sagas. Their ability to find drama in the mundane is truly an art form, leaving colleagues simultaneously amused and exasperated by the chaos they create. After all, in the world of the Crisis Connoisseur, every hiccup is a masterpiece waiting to be unveiled!

And the last one, but never the least. This species can sort of make your life hell, turning your work life upside down.

HR Intimidator

In the history of corporate folklore, the HR Intimidator is a puzzling figure, creating an atmosphere of fear and uncertainty. Team members walk on eggshells, constantly second-guessing their actions and decisions, all in the name of appeasing the mysterious forces they believe reside within the hallowed halls of Human Resources (HR).

This mysterious species thrives on creating an atmosphere of perpetual uncertainty. They drop hints about impending policy changes, organisational restructuring, or mysterious HR directives, keeping colleagues in a constant state of trepidation.

The HR intimidator poses as the emissary of the HR gods. The supervisors who have the peculiarities never miss a chance to drop mysterious hints about the secret HR meetings and the decisions, leaving the team trembling in fear of unseen consequences; they also havé a couple of supporters clinging left and right to validate and second to all that has been mentioned.

I know and realize that encountering these inscrutable people is an inevitable component of the journey. However, I have made a personal vow to evolve into a better, more compassionate version of all the aforementioned breeds and species.

In my ascension up the corporate ladder, I hope to break the cycle of HR intimidation by cultivating an environment of empathy, understanding, and true leadership. My goal is to positively impact the workplace by establishing an environment where co-workers feel supported, respected, and motivated to succeed.

I reject the concepts of cryptic communication and ambiguity in authority. Instead of instilling fear, I strive to demonstrate empathy and responsibility towards my co-workers and the organisation as a whole.

However, only time will tell whether a person's sense of morality diminishes as his or her influence grows.

"Power tends to corrupt; absolute power corrupts absolutely.".

Chapter 6:
The Emoji Enthusiast (EE): A Symphony of Symbols

The inclusion of emoticons in contemporary communication has become indispensable, providing a universal and approachable means for individuals of diverse cultural and linguistic backgrounds to establish connections and gain comprehension in the digital domain. Symbols have undergone a process of evolution to encompass a wide variety of components, such as cuisine, facial expressions, animals, and objects, thereby offering a vast array of alternatives to accommodate diverse conversations and contexts.

Paul, an average-height, slender young man with blurred vision and an eye-sight grade of 6/6, has an altogether different perspective on everything. With the proficiency that he claims to possess unparalleled knowledge of business correspondence, this individual manages his correspondence using an orchestration of emoticons that elevates the ordinary to a vivid composition of sentiments. To gain a sense of the sentiments conveyed, dear readers, it is recommended that you envision his emails as a digital canvas where each sentence is adorned with fanciful dancing figures, smiley faces, and raised thumbs. This artistic expression challenges the stoic conventions of formal communication.

Paul, in characteristically EE fashion, responded to a project deadline crisis with an email containing an abundance of rocket emoticons in the subject line—a visual introduction to anticipation and urgency. In the midst of the imminent disorder, the email's body unfolded in a melodic display of emojis, representing determination, collaboration, and a light touch of playful panic. Colleagues, taken aback by this unanticipated injection of humour, discovered themselves bursting with laughter amidst the frenzy of approaching deadlines.

In a separate occurrence, Paul inquired for managerial direction via email, commencing it with a sequence of question mark emoticons, symbolizing a ballet of ambiguity. However, beneath this visually arresting introduction, there was a thorough explanation of the circumstances, along with cleverly placed double question marks that begged for clarification. Notwithstanding the seriousness of the content, the email emanated an aura of friendliness due to the skilful incorporation of emoticons.

However, not all members of the business community are sensitive to such an emotional display in formal conversations. The flurry of emoticons initially surprised some recipients, including myself, and made us wonder if it was an accurate reflection of Paul's personality or if it was merely an attempt to hide a lack of communication skills.

The responses exhibited by the recipients of the email are as varied as a spectrum of hues. Certain individuals commend the light-hearted element, perceiving it as a revitalizing diversion from the tedium that comes with the overuse of jargon and acronyms in formal correspondence. They perceive it as an exceptional brushstroke that infuses vitality into the frequently lifeless corporate setting. On the other hand, some people might view it as a slight against professionalism or an attempt to downplay how serious the issue is.

The fundamental inquiry regarding whether these emoticons faithfully represent Paul's mental condition or function as a crutch is a matter of personal interpretation.

Those in favour contend that these symbols serve as extensions of his persona, providing insights into his emotional terrain and promoting a sense of connection. However, there are those who may harbour scepticism and doubt whether these kaleidoscopic glyphs effectively communicate the intended message or simply obscure it.

Ultimately, The Emoji Enthusiast stimulates a conversation regarding the transformation of communication in the workplace. Comparable to musical notation, emojis have the ability to imbue a sense of humanity into the inflexible corporate environment.

However, it is critical to strike the appropriate chord so that this visual symphony complements the intricate equilibrium of professional interaction rather than detracts from it.

While we continue to decipher Paul's emails with the same zeal, it is important to bear in mind that while emoticons can augment digital communication, their application should be prudent and conscientious of the possible disadvantages; this is especially true in situations that demand clarity, professionalism, and universal comprehension.

Chapter 7:
The Secret Office Romance

I hope the words and thoughts that I've shared thus far have piqued your interest and encouraged you to dig deeper. I continue to weave this story with enthusiasm and genuine curiosity, hoping to catch your imagination and elicit feelings that also reflect the complexities of love and the unpredictable nature of romance.

Before you make assumptions, I would like you to imagine this: A bustling tuck shop with the delightful aroma of freshly ground coffee and quiet chatter.

And in this most basic setting, love sparks a flame, causing a chain reaction of emotions that neither person could have predicted. It can strike at any time; no setting or location is perfect.

Love, in its most fundamental form, is an unpredictable force that defies plans and expectations. It has the extraordinary ability to bloom anywhere and at any time, shocking us and permanently changing the path of our lives. Love does not follow a script; it simply happens, uninvited and unpredictably.

Two unsuspecting co-workers have dared to go on a hidden journey of passion in the sacred halls of corporate monotony, where the hum of photocopiers and the drone of endless meetings provide the perfect setting for love. Our brave souls have decided to take the perilous route of The Secret Workplace Romance through the white-grey cubicle jungle, where love is as uncommon as a functional workplace beverage machine.

Meet Summi, a lovely data analyst with an extraordinary knack for spreadsheets and a secret obsession for romance novels. Ryan, on the other hand, defines enthusiasm as overcoming obstacles and avoiding team meetings.

Summi, with her infectious smile, and Ryan, the exuberant go-getter, were co-workers who shared much more than an office. They had no idea that their journey via work assignments, team meetings, and informal conversations would lead to their happily ever after.

Their story was a secret dance, expertly set to match the pace of office routines. The exchange of sneaky stares in meetings and snatched minutes by the coffee machine served as a quiet introduction to their budding affair. As they navigated the maze of deadlines and project reports, their friendship grew stronger, like vines intertwining in a hidden garden.

Despite their best efforts to keep their growing connection a secret, the office gossip network had other plans. Cryptic whispers and knowing glances among colleagues transformed the once-private affair into a source of interest. The office was abuzz with gossip, and co-workers exchanged knowing glances, converting water dispenser chats into cryptic conversations, as if they had transformed the workplace into a stage for a drama that only a few were aware of.

Despite hushed chatter and speculative office pool bets on when the big revelation would occur, Summi and Ryan remained covert. They devised a code of grins and nods, a silent pact to keep their love tale contained in the quiet corners of the 10th floor.

Meanwhile, as an unwitting observer in this workplace drama, I remained blissfully unaware of the burgeoning romance. Summi and Ryan, as far as I knew, were just excellent teammates who collaborated effectively on assignments. I had no notion that their unsaid language was a love story in and of itself, waiting to be told.

The unexpected news then hit the office like a thunderbolt, similar to a plot twist in a romance book. Summi and Ryan were on their way to a destination wedding. Colleagues who had been speculating for months exchanged shocked looks, and the corner conversation evolved into joyful celebrations.

The once-secret love story had turned into a full-fledged fairy tale, surprising everyone in the office. When the newlyweds returned, they were met with cheers, shouting, and a renewed appreciation for the power of love among corporate cubicles.

The revelation of the love story surprised many people, including me. Prior to this revelation, many of us assumed Ryan was already married. The unravelling of their romantic story was a delightful plot element that challenged our preconceived views while also bringing an unexpected warmth to the office dynamics.

Undoubtedly, innumerable love tales are silently happening within the cubicles, of which I continue to be blissfully unaware. Perhaps I should be more alert, partaking in the casual discussion that occurs during the beverage and breakroom conversations. However, Summi and Ryan's narrative is one to remember—a story that transcends the banal and brings delight to the typical corporate world.

As a consequence of this, the corridors and bays of the tenth floor became spectators in a love story, which serves as an illustration of the fact that the most surprising surprises are sometimes those that you do not anticipate.

Chapter 8:
The Coffee Cappers

An unexpected development occurs when co-workers band together to seize the newly introduced cold beverage machine, transforming the office lounge into the focal point of the most audacious display of caffeinated resistance in the annals of business.

Why has this uprising occurred? Ah! It is the newly installed cold beverage dispenser that has caused a commotion among the caffeine-dependent members of the office staff.

In an effort to maintain employee motivation and productivity, the organization developed a sophisticated cold beverage dispenser with the specific purpose of mitigating afternoon fatigue. However, what they failed to anticipate was that this mechanism, one frothy cup at a time, would ignite a revolution.

An enthusiastic fanfare greeted the machine's arrival, reverberating throughout the office bay and corridors. The streamlined, cutting-edge apparatus became an immediate sensation, showcasing a variety of flavours that rivalled the complexity of a rainbow. Embraced in fruit-infused carbonated concoctions and chilled lattes, it seemed as though the elixir of efficiency had at last materialized.

However, what was initially intended to be a method of revitalization quickly turned into a competition among co-workers that was fuelled by caffeine. The group of people that I referred to as the Coffee Cappers at the time, who have since become widely recognised as the Coffee Cappers community, decided to try out every variety that this machine has to offer in a single day. Even the mere idea of a flavour that has not been proven can instil a sense of pride in a person.

The initial victim was Ricky, an unfortunate intern who committed the fatal error of taking a leisurely stroll to the lounge area during his lunch break. Little did he know, the Coffee Cappers had taken possession of the vending machine. They flocked around it, creating strange caffeine-infused concoctions cup after cup in a frenzy.

Ricky observed with perplexity as an assortment of increasingly bizarre beverages was presented to him. The Mango Mocha Madness, the Berry Blast Cold Brew, and the Chai-Chocolate-Cherry-Chiller were all rather dubious. The environment in the office resembled that of a crazed scientist's laboratory; cups and beakers were all over the place.

The Coffee Cappers took turns sampling, sipping, and critiquing with the seriousness of wine connoisseurs. They vigorously debated the virtues of each flavour to the point where coffee beans would have blushed. Excessive froth! Someone would exclaim, "Not enough espresso kick!" while another would proclaim.

It became increasingly apparent that the vending machine was approaching a state of extreme fatigue as the day advanced. Gears groaned and steam hissed in response to the relentless assault of coffee-thirsty colleagues. The Coffee Cappers disregarded the ominous overheating WARNING that flashed on the machine's digital display. Without a doubt, they were determined to quench their thirst with the help of that machine.

It appeared as though the coffee machine would dissolve into thin air, sucked dry by the caffeine-thirsty swarm, as the shift neared its conclusion. The Coffee Cappers exclaimed in triumph, their eyes clouded with the insanity induced by caffeine. Having defeated the machine and sampled each flavour, they had survived to tell the tale.

Thus, the great Coffee Capper farce continues, esteemed readers. Once a haven of peace, the lounge area is now a battleground with empty cups, coffee bean shards, smears scattered about and nearly everywhere, and the remnants of discarded cups. Although the beleaguered coffee machine has managed to endure this round, its future is uncertain in regards to the culinary creations that the Coffee Cappers may devise.

Ultimately, this serves as a reminder that even a basic coffee machine can be utilized as a pawn in the caffeine-fuelled games of its users within the realm of office diversions.

With unwavering determination and courage, the Coffee Cappers continue their relentless pursuit of the perfect chilled beverage, hopping from one floor to other.

Godspeed, brave caffeine warriors.

Chapter 9:
The Trials and the Tribulations

The journey of life inevitably includes challenges and difficulties because each aspect of our existence comes with its own unique set of trials and tribulations.

So is the sparkling utopia of the corporate world, where dreams come true, although in the form of repeated nightmares about endless meetings and soul-crushing bureaucracy. We go on a fascinating adventure full of trials and tribulations, as if we were players in a warped version of the fairy tale "Corporate Hood."

The first enchantment on our list is the fascinating "Email Quest." Brace yourself as you navigate the hazardous waters of your inbox, where messages multiply like rabbits. Just when you think you've defeated the beast, a new wave appears, leaving you wondering whether you'll ever see the shores of Inbox Zero.

Behold the enchanted dance of office politics, a fascinating carnival of craziness and mind-bending tricks! A convoluted web of relationships, power struggles, and covert pecking orders that reduce industrious employees to mere players on the big chessboard of corporate instability. It's like a Classic drama, except with more spreadsheets and less monologues.

Let's not forget the tremendous excitement of meeting tight deadlines and relentlessly pursuing excellent results. It's a pressure cooker, my friends, and "work-life balance" is a mythical creature that is said to exist but is about as true as a unicorn riding a rainbow. Oh, the pleasant song of stress, singing us a lullaby of constant tiredness.

But wait—there's more!

The ever-present threat of job insecurity, that dark cloud throwing shadows over even the most dedicated employees. The incessant need to justify one's relevance in a market that changes quicker than a chameleon on roller skates may turn nights into sleepless marathons of anxiety.

Ahh, the beautiful "Performance Review Ritual." Gather 'round, dear employees, as you confront the almighty manager who holds the key to your future.

Will they lavish you with compliments, or will they send the ghosts of prior PowerPoint presentations to haunt your every career move? It's an exciting performance that keeps everyone on the edge of their ergonomic seats.

Let's not overlook the wonderful "Team Building Ceremonies." These sessions, which typically resemble a strange cross between summer camp and a low-budget reality show, are supposed to strengthen bonds among colleagues. Prepare for trust breakdowns, awkward icebreakers, and the never-ending struggle to escape being assigned the humiliating team name.

Who could really miss the delightful "Dress Code Dilemma"? As you decipher the hidden language of business casual, you'll need to strike a fine balance between professionalism and individual expression. Is wearing jeans and a nice shirt acceptable, or is it a one-way ticket to the dungeons of fashion faux pas?

In this charmed world, the coffee machine is the elixir of productivity, while the printer is a wicked sprite that enjoys paper jams. The copier is a source of frustration, and inexplicable disappearances of office supplies are prevalent, leading staff to wonder if there is a black market for Post-it notes.

Despite these issues, it is vital to recognize that the corporate sector has some positive characteristics. Pragmatically, it has the potential to be a hub for growth, learning, and fulfilment.

Working in the corporate world offers a number of advantages, one of the most crucial of which is the opportunity for both personal and professional growth. When employees take advantage of opportunities to expand their skills, participate in training programmes, and get mentoring, they can reach greater levels of success. An environment that is dynamic and stimulates intellectual curiosity can be created by exposing them to a variety of tasks and building partnerships with exceptionally talented personalities.

Additionally, the corporate environment establishes a clear path for professional progression. Employees can go up the corporate ladder by working hard, being dedicated, and planning effectively. While it is rarely given, recognition and thanks for one's achievements can be tremendously satisfying.

Moreover, the corporate environment typically promotes a culture of cooperation and collaboration. Collaboration with peers from diverse backgrounds encourages creativity and innovation. A sense of shared goals and accomplishments helps build a positive workplace atmosphere.

So, dear adventurer, as you enter the corporate jungle, remember that every spreadsheet is a quest, every boardroom meeting is a fight, and every office memo is a puzzle to be solved.

While problems are unavoidable, the benefits of personal and professional development, meaningful connections, and job success make it worthwhile. Employees can survive and thrive in this dynamic environment by learning the complexities of the corporate maze and implementing successful methods.

May your coffee be strong, your Wi-Fi connection be reliable, your sense of humour be durable, and, most importantly, your manager be the epitome of generosity during these corporate trials and tribulations.

Happy navigating!

Chapter 10:
The Acronym Avalanche

Effective communication has always had a variety of components, each of which has a specific role to play in the process of communicating ideas. The relative importance of written or spoken language to nonverbal cues like ideas, gestures, and facial expressions varies depending on the situation, the cultural norms, and the type of communication in question.

Language becomes the principal means of information transmission in many situations. Speaking or writing aloud is frequently the clearest and most straightforward way to convey ideas and thoughts. Effective verbal communication abilities can boost your self-esteem and facilitate the development of deep personal and professional connections. For the purpose of promoting mutual comprehension and guaranteeing the accurate transmission of information, language must be both compelling and clear.

In the business sector, language has a different meaning. It's not just words; it's a complex web of acronyms, euphemisms, and jargon that makes up a hidden vocabulary. Handling this language maze can be likened to reading hieroglyphics; wit, comedy, and a healthy dose of scepticism are required.

Introducing the realm of office jargon, a linguistic concoction that transforms straightforward phrases into intricate riddles. In this universe, simplicity is seen as an indication of inexperience, and clarity is sacrificed on the altar of business civility. Get ready for an exhilarating voyage through the Acronym Avalanche, where communication frequently takes the form of a dance of words with hidden meanings and decoding turns into an art.

Imagine that on a bright Monday morning, you walk into the office, well prepared and motivated to take on the difficulties of the week ahead, only to have a co-worker shout at you, "Let's touch base offline about the low-hanging fruits we need to take action." You can't help but wonder if your colleague has started a new job as a botanist or if you've just entered a fruit market.

The corporate jargon is frequently exemplified as a seemingly unintimidating discourse that becomes engulfed in phrases that border on silliness and are frequently pretentious. Furthermore, this vexatious gobbledygook has captivated the majority of the working class across the globe.

The easiest chores on the list are what are referred to as the "low-hanging fruits"—they are not really fruits at all. Furthermore, "touching base offline" is really a code word for "let's talk about it later."

Let's now explore the core of corporate linguistic complexities, where characters are combined carelessly to create acronyms that are only understandable to the well-initiated. You could become lost in a sea of alphabet soup if you're not proficient in this language, which is a language inside a language.

Here's an example: "Let's lowball the scope, circle back on the metrics during the QBR, touch the baseline with the ASAP implementation, ensure the OOO responses are within EOD, and analyse the YTD performance, but remember, don't boil the ocean on this brief— maintain a high-level approach and avoid delving too deep." This could appear to amateurs as a mysterious message from a tech-savvy alien. But fret not—I shall act as your linguistic guide.

Lowball the scope: Keep the project or assignment simple or basic rather than too complex.

Let's go back to the performance metrics from the quarterly business review (QBR) and discuss them.

To reach the baseline, apply the ASAP implementation as follows: A work or project should be implemented as soon as it is started, fulfilling any necessary prerequisites.

Verify that the OOO responses fit inside the EOD. Make sure that out-of-office answers are set up and activated at the end of the working day.

Examine and evaluate the performance statistics to analyse the year-to-date results.

For now, let's not boil the ocean. Avoid overanalysing or complicating this task; instead, make it generic and not unduly detailed.

A sharp eye and a willingness to delve into the depths of organisational linguistics are necessary for navigating the Acronym Avalanche. In this game, deciphering acronyms is similar to finding hidden treasure, and misinterpreting them might result in a hilarious series of mishaps.

Beyond acronyms, office jargon also uses euphemisms, which are like a velvet glove on a steel fist to cushion the blows of reality. When someone says, "We're in a period of right-sizing," for example, they really mean that layoffs are imminent. If a manager says, "We need to optimize our human capital," then get ready for a round of layoffs.

These language tricks drape sincerity in this strange setting and clothe delicate issues in the most exquisite euphemisms. The skill of implication is learned in this delicate ballet of words, where the silence speaks a lot louder than the words that are said.

Imagine yourself in a boardroom with people engrossed in a complex dance of buzzwords and jargon.

"Let's do a deep dive on this action item when our teams have more bandwidth. Then, we can find some synergy; meanwhile, can I also pick your brain for a few seconds and jot down the low-hanging fruits to crush them this quarter?"

Abbreviations abound, and euphemisms dance over the space like graceful ballerinas. Listening to talks about "maximising ROI," "streamlining processes," and "synergies," you may find yourself wondering if you've walked into a performance worthy of Oscar.

It becomes vital to separate content from the show in the middle of this language dance. Decisions are taken, plans are developed, and the future of initiatives is at stake in verbal gymnastics. Every word counts in this delicate dance, and it becomes an art to figure out the underlying meaning behind the elegant exterior.

Learning workplace lingo is like learning to survive in the corporate jungle if you're about to enter the workforce.

Remember these tactics as you navigate the murky waters of acronyms and euphemisms:

Be mindful of the context in which jargon is employed. Various departments or industries may have various meanings for the same abbreviation.

Never be hesitant to challenge the status quo and seek clarification when necessary. Ask someone to explain an acronym that you're not familiar with. It's possible that you're sparing yourself from nodding along to a conversation that's going too far.

Additionally, maintain a personal lexicon of acronyms and jargon that are frequently used in your company. It's a convenient reference tool that will spare you the awkward situation of misinterpreting important signals.

With its acronyms and euphemisms, office jargon is a language in and of itself. It's a language jungle where the art of seeming sophisticated frequently trumps clarity. Even though it could be easy to laugh at the ridiculousness of it all, being able to navigate and comprehend this alternate reality is a crucial ability in the business world.

That being said, the next time you're at a meeting with co-workers discussing how to "leverage synergies for a paradigm shift in the KPIs," stop and admire the verbal gymnastics.

Recall that professionals are trying to make sense of their work, initiatives, and goals behind the curtain of jargon.

It could be challenging to decipher hieroglyphics in the vast network of commercial communication. However, you may make it through and even thrive in the intricate dance of workplace jargon if you add a little satire, a little comedy, and a little scepticism.

Greetings from the language jungle! I hope you continue to have good decoding skills!

Chapter 11:
Conjunctivitis Survivor

A manager in this peculiar circus serves as the equivalent of a ringmaster. They adeptly handle expectations, enforce strict deadlines, and master the skill of maintaining subordinates on edge. They navigate office politics with the delicacy of a diplomat, the tenacity of a saint, and the guile of a chess prodigy. A manager assumes the role of a maestro, overseeing the corporate cordiality to guarantee flawless performance of each note, even if it entails quietly manipulating a few strings.

Although I had a passing familiarity with the managerial tightrope routine, which is a common occurrence in the business world, I failed to grasp its nuances, possibly because I had thus far been spared the full intensity of the experience. My approach to work has consistently been characterized by attention to detail: I have persistently met deadlines and effectively communicated plans and notifications for leaves (with the exception of those flare-ups and unanticipated circumstances involving the chronic autoimmune-related illness that I am plagued with and it disrupt this well-coordinated dance: uninvited guests who land and announce their arrival without making an effort to RSVP). I am relieved to say that my conduct and disciplinary record have remained impeccable since my infancy, owing to the influence of my parents in my life and, naturally, my upbringing.

On a lovely Monday morning (naah, I am not plagued or petrified of those common Monday blues; rather, I feel super energised), zeal sprouting to a new level to keep myself afloat for the week ahead, I boarded the cab and found myself sharing the cab with co-workers from different teams within the same towering edifice. We exchanged greetings and checked for well-being, and any updates since we last met, which was on Friday of the previous week.

In keeping with my custom, I immersed myself in the captivating realm of "The Palace of Illusions," a literary work authored by Chitra Banerjee that holds a special place in my heart—an extraordinary feminist retelling of an epic tale that explores depths of emotion, strength, frailty, honour, and humiliation—while simultaneously enjoying the calming melodies emanating from my headphones.

Little did I know that this voyage would evolve into an anecdote concerning the intricacies of the workplace and astute manoeuvring. As the stage was set with materials for a light-hearted performance of power plays, I found myself in the audience, bewildered and completely engrossed in literature and music.

As we proceeded with our weekly commute, the cab transformed into a dramatic environment featuring Sonia, an experienced colleague in the fraud department. It was as though we were actors in a prelude, we exchanged pleasantries to set the tone for the subsequent act.

In this compelling drama, Sonia's phone rang, signalling the arrival of Anita via video call, her long-time partner on the battlefield of office politics. Anita, who woke up with swollen, red, and watery eyes, sought Sonia's counsel regarding the age-old dilemma of whether to courageously confront the corporate firing squad or just announce your sickness due to the widespread conjunctivitis. The itching in her eye exacerbated her discomfort, but this illness and pain represented a metaphor for a day off rather than merely a physical ailment.

Sonia suggested that she engage in a video conference with her manager to discuss the optimal course of action while maintaining complete composure; it would be beneficial if she allowed herself a few tears to roll down her cheeks during the conversation.

The purpose of this action was to compel the manager to grant her a medical leave, during which she would be obligated to continue to work remotely from the comfort of her home.

From a rudimentary perspective, I have consistently believed that managers possess the ability to effectively navigate the precipice of an organisation. However, I was not well-informed regarding the extent of their capabilities, as I had never personally encountered them. As a result of my spotless record, I have been shielded from their astute tactics.

Anita's performance was flawless, following in the footsteps of Sonia's great direction during the production. The act was made more dramatic by the torrential tears that were shed, as if being performed as an encore at a tragic opera. To everyone's surprise, the management acquiesced to the theatre and authorised medical leave and work-from-home privileges.

It eluded my understanding that this incident represented not a solitary occurrence but rather a pervasive epidemic—not of conjunctivitis instead an astute office politics. Colleagues from different floors were compelled to carry out comparable deeds in accordance with the malevolent notion of anchor days—those days when medical documents had to be presented at the inquisition or their presence in the office was mandatory.

Consequently, the managers wielded a formidable tool: an unquenchable thirst for evidence coupled with the capacity to maintain us on the precarious edge of the organizational abyss. An intricate tapestry of workplace drama ensued, a comedic mishap tinged with tragedy, as each of us inadvertently participated as characters in the grand spectacle of corporate foolishness.

Within this strange environment, the manager takes on the combined roles of puppeteer and puppet, synchronised with the strings of corporate madness.

However, an intriguing question pervades the narrative: why do managers appear to relish complicating the most fundamental tasks? Is it a sadistic enjoyment of authority, or do they inherit an unexplainable penchant for complexity comparable to the traits of a mother-in-law? The riddle of administrative decision-making is revealed before my eyes.

The correlation between managers and the infamous mother-in-law archetype is an intriguing finding. Both appear to operate on a command-and-control dynamic, displaying their dominance with an air of authority that occasionally crosses over into a galaxy of bizarre pleasure.

Could it be that their shared excitement originates from the command they have? It's a sadistic pleasure to watch subordinates navigate the complicated web of expectations, deadlines, and unspoken rules. Perhaps it's the satisfaction of seeing others follow their lead, a subtle allusion to the age-old saying, "I suffered; now it's your turn."

Chapter 12:
Gossip Mongers: The Unsung Heroes of Corporate Hilarity

Where boredom and spreadsheets threaten to eliminate the vibrant colour from our lives, leaving us lethargic and agitated, there is a group of unsung heroes: the Gossip Mongers (GM). Yes, you heard it correctly! Those office magpies who flutter around the pantry and coffee maker, chirping and chattering away with the latest corporate jungle news.

Believe it or not, these feathered couriers are the team's lifeblood, serving as a live webcast news channel for the entire floor. If they go missing, who will entertain the rest of the team with delicious nuggets that make the day a little less mundane?

It was a typical Tuesday morning as employees settled into their cubicles, armed with much-needed liquid courage and a weary sense of determination, and you were diligently typing away to glory on your keyboard, immersed in the riveting world of spreadsheets and deadlines, when suddenly, a hushed murmur began to permeate through the office air. The unmistakable sound of the gossip grapevine alerts you that the workplace storytellers are in operation.

The gossip mongers tip-toed into the bay, weaving through the maze of workstations like mischievous office elves, laden with the latest and greatest from the mighty corporate rumour mill.

While some may claim that gossip is simply an unnecessary distraction that impedes productivity, let me tell you something esteemed readers: gossip mongers are the secret sauce that flavours the otherwise bland soup of office life. They are the live wires of entertainment, the flavour that boosts everyday experiences to the extraordinary.

A couple of days ago, the office was humming with excitement. The gossip mongers had unearthed a frightening yarn concerning the mysterious disappearance of the last slice of birthday cake from the communal fridge. The rumour travelled like wildfire, and the break room swiftly turned into an impromptu courtroom drama.

Suspicions were raised, alliances formed, and all eyes were on Jane from the Accounting team, the main suspect in this cake-related incident, for it was confirmed by the GM team that she was the last seen at the crime scene. The gossip mongers had accidentally transformed the workplace into a captivating episode of a culinary mystery. The air was thick with suspense, and the water dispensers served as an unofficial confessional booth where staff could discuss their beliefs and concerns.

As the story unfolded, it became clear that the cake was more than a treat; it represented unity and hope in the midst of office politics. The gossip mongers had accidentally turned a commonplace event into an epic tale, with Jane's innocence or guilt serving as the focal point of the entire incident.

Many stories and assumptions were conveyed, and numerous blame games were performed. Finally, the cleaning crew mistook the cake for an abandoned and stale piece; as any of the teams had not claimed it until the EOD, they disposed it off, eliciting a collective sigh of relief. However, the gossip mongers remained undeterred. They had created a narrative that went beyond the mundane, demonstrating that even the most trivial events may become legendary when filtered through the appropriate corporate gossip lens.

I frequently wonder what the world would be like without these rumour mongers. The beverage dispenser and coffee corner would be little more than hydration stations, and the breakroom would be filled with chewing sounds rather than the enthusiastic narration that lifts simple events to epic dimensions. The office would be a silent, lifeless place, devoid of the lively stories that gossip mongers bring to light.

So, the next time you roll your eyes at the break room or lounge chatter, remember that these storytellers are the forgotten icons of workplace humour. They transform the ordinary into the extraordinary, one scandalous story at a time, and without them, the office would be a much duller place.

Cheers to the gossip mongers, the live broadcast news channel for the floor, and the true entertainers of the corporate circus!

Chapter 13:
Job Interviews: The Theatrical Spectacle of Corporate Courtship

The illustrious stage where prospective candidates, dressed in their finest attire, don their metaphorical armour and kick off on a journey to impress stone-faced interviewers sat behind a big table, eyes fixed at you with a mixture of intrigue and suspicion. It's the real-world equivalent of a reality check, a theatrical extravaganza in which you are the centre of attention. The screenplay is written in a language that is a mix of Shakespearean writing and corporate buzzwords, but the true meaning is difficult to grasp.

The first act begins with the expected query, "Tell us about yourself." Ah, the classic opener—a trap disguised as an opportunity to tell your life story. Do you keep to professional accolades, or do you indulge in your passion for looping grandiose words to give a memoir with excessive knitting? It's a very fine line between appearing amazing and sympathetic—tightrope walks worthy of Cirque du Soleil (the largest Canadian entertainment company and the largest contemporary circus producer in the world).

And there you go—delivering the robotic monologue with carefully chosen industry buzzwords commences with some succinctly stated facts and data. A soliloquy in which you glorify your virtues, sing praises for your accomplishments, and gently indicate that you can save the company from the impending doom on your own. Set aside your modesty; now is your moment to shine, and shine you will, like a supernova in the corporate galaxy.

However, beware of the traps of the humblebrag, which is the art of boasting while wearing a thin cloak of modesty. "Oh, the project? It was just a minor project I worked on over the weekend." Translation: I am the modern-day Da Vinci, and my weekend initiatives outperform the entire company's strategic plan.

Now comes the interrogation, a rapid-fire round in which questions are thrown at you like tomatoes in a food fight.

"Where do you see yourself in five years?" Ah, the crystal ball inquiry, which necessitates insight that even Nostradamus would envy. Do you say you're unsure or tell a story about climbing the corporate ladder faster than a superhero scaling skyscraper?

And dare not forget the behavioural questions, which are designed to get your deepest, darkest secrets and to extent also decide your future.

"Tell us about a time you faced a challenge." Translation: Confess your workplace misdeeds, and we will determine the harshness of your penance.

As the interview progresses (and you are dissected layer by layer and bit by bit), you find yourself doing some imitation—the subtle skill of becoming the person the corporation wants you to be.

"Do you value teamwork? "Why, teamwork is my middle name!" you shout, foolishly forgetting that your real middle name is desperate Dan.

At that moment, you undergo a transformation that is like that of a chameleon, adjusting to the colours of the company culture while simultaneously fighting the need to break into the actual song and dance. After all, there is no better way to demonstrate that you are a "team player" than by performing the Macarena in the middle of a serious discussion about quarterly projections.

You are left with the cliff-hanger at the end of the interview, which is the time when the interviewers ask you if you have any questions. The interview has finally reached its climax.

Take care! When you do that, you open a door into the unknown and have the chance to demonstrate your curiosity without appearing overly eager or uneducated. When you inquire, "What is the culture of the company like?" you feel overwhelmed with anxiety, hoping that they will not respond with, "Well, it's like a dysfunctional family with a love for awkward silences."

Oh, my goodness, how could I have overlooked the most vital component: The sole purpose of this quintessential act is the pay negotiation. A dance in which each step could determine the course of your financial future. Do you aim high and run the danger of seeming crazy, or do you try to lowball yourself into a job that is good for your budget? It's a delicate ballet in which your financial worth hangs in the balance, and one wrong move could result in a symphony of wasted possibilities.

As the curtain lowers on this theatrical extravaganza, you leave the stage feeling both relieved and uncertain about what lies ahead.

The job interview, which is both a reality check and a humorous play, reminds you that in the business world, you're not just an employee; you're also a performer, an entertainer figuring out how to move up in your career.

Therefore, my dear job seekers, as you ace your next interview, I hope your responses are as polished as a recently waxed stage floor, your lines clear and concise, and your modest brags nuanced. You, my friend, are the star of the show, and the job interview is just one act in the vast spectacle that is corporate life.

And to those extremely driven people who want to move up the ladder, I wish you many more stages like these where you can give a show that would make Meryl Streep blush.

Meanwhile, I will choose my moves and manoeuvre wisely because every interview is a chance to showcase my unique talent for balancing on the tightrope of professional absurdity.

Break a leg, or better yet, break the mould!

Chapter 14:
The Multitasking Marvel: Juggling Genius or Overworked Superhero?

In today's fast-paced world, whether corporate or otherwise, where time is money and efficiency reigns supreme, where deadlines dangle like trapeze swings and meetings perform acrobatic feats, there exists a peculiar act that has everyone applauding and wincing at the same time:

multitasking, which has become the emblem of productivity. Colleagues proudly wear their multitasking capes, believing they can manage an excessive number of activities all at once.

However, beneath the surface of productivity, there is a satirical truth that calls into question the fundamental core of this corporate fiction. From the tremendous performances of this circus, two figures emerge as the show's stars: Multitask Maestro Garvit (liked to be called Gary) and Zen Master Bonnie.

While I prepare you for the grand comparison between Bonnie and Gary, both as different as they can be, like day and night, these two individuals embody stark contrasts, with personalities as distinct as the poles on a magnet.

I'd like you to imagine an entirely different way of multitasking: you're in a meeting, nodding earnestly at your boss's presentation while covertly drafting an email response in your head, mentally composing a grocery list, and plotting your escape to the restroom, where you can take a breather and scroll through social media to reset your mind. This, my dear readers, is not simply multitasking, but a corporate version of mental gymnastics that we all engage in on a regular basis.

Our corporate monarchs appear to want us to become human Swiss Army knives capable of doing as many tasks as one could and all at once. "Can you analyse reports, organize a team-building activity, and train rookies? "Oh, and make it snappy—time is money!" they declare, as if time were a physical commodity like a chocolate bar.

But lest we forget about the actual multitasking heroes: those who are able to toggle between things with the ease of a caffeinated squirrel on a pogo stick. They are the folks who answer emails during Zoom meetings, sign off on documents with one hand while stirring their soup with the other, and respond to Slack messages before they are even sent. If there were an Olympic event for multitasking, these individuals would take home gold medals, and we'd all be left speechless at their ability to defy the laws of time and rationality.

Let's take a satirical stroll around the chaotic cubicles and explore these two fascinating specimens in their native environment.

Our protagonist, Gary, is the Multitask Maestro. Gary believes he is the most efficient person in the world due to his mastery of multitasking. He is always armed with a laptop, smartphone, and a coffee mug with an espresso intravenous (IV) line. His desk resembles a spaceship cockpit, and he moves his fingers over the keyboard like a professional pianist. He has never missed a deadline, has no records of SLA compromised ever, has no shrinkage in his team ever, and is always up and about for any challenges coming his way.

His colleagues think that although Gary appears busy, he is on the verge of a caffeine-fuelled meltdown. Gary appears placid on the surface but is actually like a duck paddling fast under the water, he struggles arduously to maintain buoyancy.

Zen Master Bonnie, who embodies the concept of "chillax," stands out from the corporate circus. Bonnie is an expert at staying calm in a hectic environment. His desk is decorated with tranquil succulents, and the background of his computer screen is a serene sunset (Windows11 template screensaver, which he keeps changing with the change in his mood). Gary is racing through his work, while Bonnie relaxes, drinks herbal tea, exchanges wise words with peers, and mulls over the cryptic communications from upper management, always ready with a reckoner when questioned. Bonnie views meetings as an opportunity to practice, preach, and teach mindfulness, rather than a war to be won.

As these two titans meet in the business jungle, it's a showdown to match any legendary duel. With his many screens and caffeine exuberance, Gary meets off against Bonnie, who has a calm demeanour and an incredible ability to identify the eye of the storm.

And in this mundane fiesta, who wins?

The Multitask Maestro and the Zen Master can coexist in the vast show of the business world. Whether you are juggling duties with Gary's flair or embracing chaos with

Bonnie's calm, the goal is to discover your own beat in this symphony of spreadsheets and cacophony of Slack messages. After all, the corporate circus is nothing more than a high-stakes, caffeine-fuelled extravaganza in which everyone is basically trying not to trip over their own two feet—or, in Gary's case, stumble on their many screens.

In this multitasking dystopia, working longer hours and going above and beyond the call of duty are considered badges of honour. The workplace requires skill in one's role as well as a constant readiness to take action at the drop of the hat. The adoption of burnout culture and the "always on" mentality reinforces the notion that a true professional is one who sacrifices personal time and well-being for the sake of the organization.

As we traverse this brave new world of multitasking mayhem, the distinction between dedication and self-destruction becomes blurred. The once-clear borders between work and home life have blurred, leaving employees wondering whether they are truly thriving or simply surviving.

To add a layer of irony to this corporate drama, consider the studies that show the negative effects of continuous multitasking, such as lower cognitive performance, higher stress, and an increased risk of errors. The office becomes a pressure cooker, and the multitasking maven unconsciously simmers in overcommitments.

In the never-ending search for excellence over perfection, perhaps it's time to reassess the multitasking myth. Instead of rewarding those who can handle a large number of jobs concurrently, let us appreciate the efficiency of focus and the art of single-tasking. A highly effective worker may not have a dozen tabs open on their browser but rather approaches things systematically, one at a time.

Dear corporate warriors, as we manage our different professional commitments, let's take a moment to enjoy the craziness of it all. Perhaps, in our pursuit of multitasking expertise, we've neglected the simple satisfaction of concentrating on one activity at a time—a revolutionary thought that could catch on.

Until then, let us celebrate the multitaskers, the unsung heroes of the corporate circus who spin plates and answer emails with a smile—all in a day's work.

Cheers to wonderful chaos!

Chapter 15:
Office Meetings: The Black Hole of Productivity

Corporate meetings: an expertly planned dance of professional pretence in which people congregate, usually with some restlessness in their body language and relentlessness on their faces, to debate topics of great significance that have already been addressed in the secret lair of higher-ups. It is the adult version of gathering around a magic eight ball, except instead of shaking it, you shuffle through a fancy PowerPoint presentation.

In this mysterious ritual, participants engage in a symphony of head nods, handshakes, and the occasional furrowed brow, all while pretending that the outcome is not as predictable as the workplace coffee choices. Faking astonishment at the facts you heard in the pre-meeting briefing is a delicate art, like a company of highly skilled actors doing a Broadway production named "The Illusion of Decision-Making."

These meetings are linguistic puzzles in which the goal is not to comprehend but to energetically nod along, hoping no one notices your mind wandering off into thoughts of a three-day weekend and the next holiday you need to plan.

Despite the glorious setting, the underlying objective of these events is to allow everyone to formally agree to disagree without actually raising any issues. It's a diplomatic circus, with the tightrope walkers being middle managers who must delicately balance not to upset the status quo while simultaneously pretending to contribute.

Amidst the white and grey-coloured walls and spotless glass dividers that seemed to stretch into eternity, there stood a man - exactly five feet and eight inches tall. He had a gruff temperament and rigid body language. His posture was flawless; he stood solid and unwavering, like a sentinel guarding the kingdom's good, bad, and ugly secrets. His arrogance clung to him like a meticulously tailored business suit, exuding authority and commanding respect despite verbal tug-of-war and recurrent confrontations within the concrete battlefield.

His sharp and perceptive eyes appeared to scan the office landscape with critical accuracy, missing no detail in his pursuit of organizational perfection, each wrinkle on his face revealing a story of innumerable arguments and strategic manoeuvres.

His enthusiasm for meetings knew no bounds. Sir Drudgery, as he was lovingly nicknamed by the team, believed in the power of long (never-ending) meetings, where time seemed to stretch like taffy and productivity vanished into a black hole of nothingness.

Every meeting would become an overwhelming spectacle in the name of colleague involvement, a symphony of jargon blending with threats and HR intimidation, creating an ecology with the intensity of a Shakespearean tragedy. As the hour crept down, colleagues gripped their chairs, wondering whether a breakout was a faraway fantasy.

In the absence of any discernible agenda, the conferences danced through the geographical regions of ambiguity, leaving contributors to decipher the cryptic messages hidden within Sir Drudgery's grandiloquent speeches, "Synergy"; he'd exclaim, as the team exchanged at a loss for words glances, uncertain if they were discussing a business strategy or summoning historical spirits.

As the hours passed, a few unfortunate folks with weak stomachs found themselves unintentionally disclosing things they'd promised to keep to their graves. Sir Drudgery, who had an amazing ability to extract unintentional confessions, relished the unexpected revelations, transforming the conference room into a confessional booth for corporate crimes.

However, the big display did not end with the final threat or term. Oh no! Sir Drudgery, in an astonishing turn of events, would demand the meeting minutes, as if he intended to submit them for the Pulitzer Prize in Literature. The poor soul assigned as the note-taker would race to capture the main points of the meeting, attempting to make sense of the convoluted debates that took place.

The sessions, which began with a goal that was as unobtainable as a unicorn, eventually came to an end. The team emerged dizzy and confused, unsure whether the previous hour had been a fever dream or a business séance. The minutes of the meetings were now archived in the possession of Lord Sir Drudgery, along with other otherworldly belongings that only he could comprehend.

Consequently, the tradition of Sir Drudgery's meetings continued and was narrated; expert critics were surreptitiously passed by employees over water dispensers and everywhere else to vent out.

One thing was certain as they ventured into the uncharted territories of their workdays: the buzzword-fuelled black hole of productivity would always be on the horizon, ready to gorge time and sanity in its hungry jaws.

May you be blessed with the dexterity to take care of much of the donkey work and brace yourself for a marathon of endless meetings and phone calls that rivals the stamina.

Chapter 16:
The Whimsical World of MT:
Mandatory Training

Salutations, fellow men and women in the corporate arena! You are in for a delight if you have ever contemplated how those dazzling promotions gracefully glide across the horizon. Anticipate a thrilling exploration into the mysterious realm of mandatory training, which is purportedly the means to progress within an organisational structure.

In the land of cubicles, a novel practice has emerged: the art of cross-skilling and upskilling. In fact, esteemed colleagues, it has been rumoured that compulsory training sessions elevate commoners to the status of promotion eligible wizards—magical spells of the twenty-first century. As we commence this jovial expedition, put on your wizard hats (or fashionable scarves, ladies, should you be concerned about ruining your hairstyles).

Consider yourself an unsuspecting professional, seated in a well-illuminated space where a PowerPoint magus chants benevolent rituals, extolling the advantages of enhancing your skill set. A dense perfume permeates the surroundings with the aroma of freshly brewed enthusiasm, as if the mere aroma might enhance our cognitive abilities and elevate us to the position of celebrities.

Excel proficiency is the first item of instruction that is included in the curriculum. There is no need to be concerned because the training wizard assures you that you will be able to effortlessly change your tables and find solutions to your problems. Apparently, to us, the ability to control cells could perhaps serve as the way to acquire access to the executive lavatory and possibly even to the kitchen as well (much like Donna Paulsen has unrestricted access to the manager's magnificent kitchen), which represents the pinnacle of corporate rank.

As we progress through the mandatory training, we are being compelled to acquire a wide range of skills, much like circus performers in a professional environment. The aspirants will be transformed into wordsmiths of the highest calibre if we are successful in achieving our goal of being proficient in email diplomacy. This will ensure that our digital correspondences are as captivating as sonnets written by William Wordsworth. Following that, we will interpret the obscure language of office vernacular, an aptitude considered indispensable for individuals striving to achieve greater heights on the professional trapeze.

Do not rush; there is more! Attend the workshop, which is purely devoted to emotional intelligence, which is a potentially transformational elixir that will elevate us to the level of workplace alchemists who can change our co-workers' frowns into smiles. "Embrace the dissatisfied colleague with the affection of a thousand positive vibes; have no fear of them," the training magus whispered. "They are not to be feared."

In the big finale, we emerge from the training chambers with freshly acquired powers and armed with certifications that are comparable to a wizard's diploma. We are now prepared to conquer the corporate empire. The time has come for the promotion! Indeed, we believed so.

The revelation comes about when the circumstances come to an end: promotions are as hazy as the last drop of coffee that is poured into the shared pot. There is a possibility that our recently gained powers are nothing more than fantasies or that our lack of experience amused the celestial creatures that oversee promotions.

This satirical exploration of the arbitrary realm of mandatory training establishes a singular truth: the trajectory towards advancement is a merry anecdote, where the true power is not derived from acquired proficiencies but rather from the companionship cultivated as we mingle in the training halls, forge alliances, exchange witty banter, and create an invisible web of influence. It appears that knowing who knows you is equally as important as knowing what you know when it comes to promotion.

However, as we make our way through this maze of mandated training and upskilling, the issue that keeps popping up like a lingering spell is whether or not the acquisition of skills actually guarantees the promotion that we so desperately want or whether or not we are caught up in the illusion of progress.

It is possible that upskilling is the shining outfit in the vast cosmic ballet of promotions; however, the performance is the show's true star. Applying these skills, demonstrating your wizardry in tasks and projects, and leaving a trail of excellence is the magic that can turn the limelight towards the promotion stage. This is the ability that can shift the spotlight towards the promotion stage.

Therefore, dear corporate enchanters, when you embark on the road of mandated training and upskilling, keep in mind that the true alchemy lies not just in the acquisition of skills but in the utilisation of those skills to create a symphony of success. Additionally, who knows? Perhaps, just possibly, that letter of promotion is the enchanted treasure that is waiting for you at the end of the rainbow in the corporate ecosphere.

Chapter 17:
From Pipeline to Potluck: The Triumph of Team Feast

A communal gathering called potluck, where each participant contributes a dish of food, often homemade, to be shared among the group. In a potluck, the responsibility for preparing and bringing food is distributed among the attendees, creating an eclectic spread of dishes; the dishes brought by individuals are not predetermined or planned in advance. Instead, it's a spontaneous and varied collection of foods brought by different participants, creating a diverse and often unpredictable (perhaps that is why it is a potluck) feast.

Ah, this epic potluck tale, a culinary voyage that took nearly a year to negotiate the death-defying waters of planning purgatory. The potluck idea simmered in the pipeline, threatening to become a five-year plan—a fate worse than being served with overcooked spaghetti.

But lo and behold! With the start of a new period defined by a shift in team structure and the new year's optimism, where exuberance beats procrastination, a brave volunteer emerged. This eager soul, powered by the flames of passion, resolved to seize the spatula of destiny and take command.

Undeterred by the ghosts of previous potluck plans, our culinary hero accepted the task of bringing the concept to reality. She took on the daunting task of organising the potluck bonanza with the accuracy of a seasoned chef and the attention to detail of a Michelin-starred planner.

The project life cycle, once a whisper in the hallways of bureaucratic indecision, now stands tall and proud, meticulously defined. No detail was overlooked, from the first brainstorming session on potluck themes to the complexities of sign-up papers for dish contributions.

The team was excited as the passionate volunteer juggled the pots and pans of project management. The potluck, which had become a beacon of optimism and gastronomic delight, was no longer a distant fantasy but rather an actual reality that would soon unfold in the workplace breakroom.

Now begins the part of the project that most people think of as the project: executing the tasks, deliverables, and milestones—date, time, and venue—all defined as the culinary carnival in the corporate circus where Tupperware and Borosil battles were waged and the office microwave became a battleground of aromatic delights. The well-seasoned casserole was simmering its way into the heart of the corporate office, bringing with it a buffet of camaraderie and culinary chaos.

The freshly renovated pantry stood as a gastronomic wonderland, with each dish resembling either a meticulously created masterpiece or a gallant attempt at culinary heroics.

The aroma drifting through the air was more than just the smell of sumptuous food; it was an intoxicating fragrance of team spirit, simmering collaboration, and a touch of friendly competition.

Will Kiran's excellent Gajar Halwa and Rabri surpass Deep's unconventional Shahi Paneer? The breakroom turned into a gastronomic battlefield, with the microwave serving as a strategic outpost for reheating dominance.

And how can I dare to forget the unstated potluck hierarchy? The courageous colleagues who tackle the delicate art of soufflés and caramel pudding rise to the top of the potluck hierarchy, while the cautious providers of store-bought cookies and cupcakes find their position in dessert democracy.

As the time to launch the project potluck approached, the office erupted into a potluck frenzy. Colleagues gathered around the table like hungry wolves, examining the buffet with a mixture of expectation and shrewd calculation. This potluck was more than simply a meal; it was a feast of social interaction, with process update talks replaced by debates over the advantages and returns of homemade vs. store-bought.

And as we applaud the heroic efforts of the potluck champion, let this tale serve as a reminder that even the most ambitious projects, marinating in the pipeline of procrastination, can find their moment to shine. But also, beware, dear reader, of the potluck hazards. The pernicious game of office politics can rear its head. A snide remark about Sara's potato salad's saltiness or an unintentional eyeroll at Bonnie's vegan lasagne attempt can result in social isolation or, worse, being assigned the office's least favourite duty for weeks.

Despite the gastronomic squabbles and the occasional battle over the last piece of pizza, the team potluck celebrates variety. It combines different flavours, ethnicities, and culinary eccentricities. The potluck, with gluten-free cookies and lactose-free casseroles, exemplifies the tapestry of tastes that comprise the corporate mosaic.

So, as you navigate the potluck landscape in your own corporate kitchen, remember that it's not just about the food—it's about the laughter shared over a well-seasoned dish, the camaraderie forged in the breakroom trenches, and the unspoken agreement that, despite the occasional potluck faux pas, we're all on this culinary adventure together.

May your potlucks be plentiful, your sign-up sheets overflow and your office kitchen forever echo with the laughter of shared culinary adventures.

Bon appétit, courageous potluck pioneers!

Chapter 18:
The Quagmire of Workplace Credit Hogs

In a world where jargon is our daily bread and coffee is the elixir of life-liquid courage and where egos compete for dominance and recognition is the elusive golden ticket, there exists a peculiar species that is famously referred to as the "Credit Hog."

These mysterious beings survive on the misfortunes of their co-workers, consuming the recognition that belongs to others and that they well deserve. Esteemed readers, accompany me on an exciting voyage that will take us through the bustling streets of corporate- the untamed territory, where Credit Hogs are free to roam in this terrain, and fair acknowledgement is as uncommon as finding someone who possesses common sense.

I come across these credit-stealing maestros more often than I would care to confess while navigating the labyrinth of this smartness-infested corporate tinsel town.

Just lately, I came across a person who possessed such a character. Although I am not a benign sage, I have a tendency to liberally share the pearls of wisdom and recommendations for process improvement with my colleagues whom I have trained. Put another way, it was like giving candy to toddlers—sweet, well-intentioned advice to help them navigate the treacherous terrain of tasks.

The Credit Hog emerged from the shadows during our monthly company update meeting, where we shared stories of victories and tragedies. As luck would have it, the credit hog was at the forefront of the conversation. This person is bursting with enthusiasm to seize the spotlight and become the name on the wall of fame. They exuded a sense of grandiosity as they narrated the ideas and recommendations I had shared with the team throughout the training sessions. It appeared as though they had discovered the renowned treasure trove and taken possession of it entirely for themselves.

I experienced a brief disruption while I was virtually present at the session, much like how an unexpected spell would catch a magician off guard. Nevertheless, the charm quickly dissipated, and in the spirit of brotherhood, I took pleasure in boisterous laughter with my comrades, who were already aware of the secret. The Credit Hog's attempt to steal had been unsuccessful, and the laughter that was enchanted spread throughout the entire digital world.

On the other hand, this should not be a reason for fear because facing a Credit Hog requires the dexterity and agility of a dragon. In order to achieve mastery over the intricate mechanisms of office politics, it is necessary to possess competence and strike a careful balance between unwavering opposition and kindness. To discover the secret operations of the hog, one should determine whether they should move cautiously, fearing a credit avalanche, or patiently wait for the appropriate chance to do so.

Imagine, even if only for a few minutes, a situation in which you are the one who makes the mistake rather than the one who is the victim. Have you ever made a dishonest claim to credit that, in fact, did not belong to you? The process of identifying persons who are worthy of credit within the intricate realm of corporate authorship can be as challenging as traversing Fairy Meadows Road, which is characterised by unstable gravel roads, perilous heights, and tight curves. The environment is characterised by a hazy landscape, where effective communication strategies in meetings and the individuals who save client relationships during challenging times are concealed.

Having said that, in light of the challenging path and terrain, it is imperative that we move with caution to avoid the potential risks associated with office politics and credit hunters. It is possible to prevent conflicts or pursue them with strategic dexterity, which is comparable to the agility of a dragon. A conversation or communication that is deliberately structured or written with sensitivity may achieve great outcomes despite the fact that a breath of fire might not be acceptable in a professional situation.

Throughout the various commercial environments, each and every one of us has undoubtedly encountered a substantial number of competitors who engage in the practice of hoarding credit. However, worry and concern are needless because each human contains the tenacious spirit of a dragon. We have successfully surmounted barriers and escaped unscathed, our figurative scales shining with the light of success. This is analogous to the fabled beings we have encountered.

They have the power to turn even the most collaborative projects into solo performances, leaving the rest of us clapping and cheering from the side-lines, like an enthralled crowd at a one-man show, or simply observing the spectacle of them soaking in the spotlight they've gleefully stolen. Trying to work with a credit hog is like attempting to tango with a ghost; you never know if they're real or a figment of your imagination.

Consequently, my esteemed comrades, you should not be afraid of the Credit Hog in the business jungle. Having intelligence, humour, and the ability to roar when it is required to assert one's proper place in the sphere of recognition are all vital qualities to possess to live in this jungle.

May steadfast fortitude stand by your side as a constant companion in the upcoming challenges. May you continue to expertly negotiate the complications, employing stubbornness as a means of fortification and resolution as an armament to guarantee that the mysterious golden ticket remains in your possession.

Chapter 19:
Perks and Quirks: Unveiling the Enigma

Where murmurs of employee benefits echo like ancient chants, there lurks a sacred artwork known as the Employee Benefits Document, which is an enigma wrapped in the eloquence of ambiguity—a scroll of aspirations, a parchment of assurances, and an inexhaustible source of merriment. Participate with me in this light-hearted and poignant demonstration as we explore the paradoxical domain of workplace privileges and peculiarities.

That sacred document scripted in the most extravagant words, the Employee Benefits Document, which guarantees the moon and stars, or a reasonable replica if not that. As we prepare ourselves to delve into the uncharted realm of "Perks and Quirks," the initial commandment is explicitly stated: "You shall have an unrestricted provision of caffeinated delights." However, despite this assurance, the coffee machine's seemingly endless supply is contingent upon the office supply budget—a budget that is equally as implausible as the Fountain of Caffeine.

With the divine mandate of complimentary access to the lounge and play area, the employees undertake an endeavour to transform their bodies into a work of art made of marble. They are oblivious to the fact that entry to the play area is subject to certain restrictions, the most prominent of which is an implicit requirement for an additional eight hours in a day to actually visit the TT and foosball table.

Nevertheless, the benefits document also guarantees an abundance of health insurance benefits. Dental, vision, and all sorts of healing (mental, physical, and emotional)— it's all there! Naturally, this is the case until one scrutinises the fine print and ascertains that the magical protection is comparable to a rudimentary magical cloak. Insurance companies detest the dreaded "exclusions" section, in which even the most harmless conditions are transformed into monstrous beasts.

And ah! the temptation of "Performance Bonuses" — a heavenly body within the document's constellation that shines with the promise of financial prosperity. However, as one progresses through the cosmic writing, the gravitational pull of ambiguity becomes apparent, casting doubt on the specifics of the bonus criterion and allowing the reader to wonder about the cosmic balance of corporate reward schemes.

Let us now discuss the magnificence of the office environment. The benefits document praises ergonomic chairs, panoramic views, and standing workstations. Nevertheless, the actual situation can be analogous to a game of musical chairs, in which the acquisition of a comfortable seat is a calculated manoeuvre involving office thrones, and panoramic views are limited to the brave souls perched near the windows—the chosen ones, gazing up at the kingdom of neighbouring office buildings.

Vacation days are regarded as sacrosanct leave granted to the weary workforce. The document highlights assurances of a copious harvest, an overabundance, and the opulence of leisure. However, in their pursuit to recoup their vacation gains, workers become entangled in a complex network of approvals, time constraints, and an enigmatic procedure that demands the relinquishment of a notarized authorization slip from the HR Gods and the office pet goldfish.

However, caution should be exercised when succumbing to the allure of this musical number—for once the ink has dried on the employment contract, the orchestration of commitments frequently transforms into an erratic tune that echoes through the corridors of dashed hopes.

In the due discourse, we shall explore the elusive notion of flexible work hours, a prospect as divine as the early morning mist. During the negotiation process, human resources assures you that the office door serves as a gateway to temporal freedom and that the clock is merely a suggestion.

However, upon commencing your exploration of flexible scheduling, you discover that the office door serves more as a symbolic gesture than a gateway to freedom, and that the clock does, in fact, employ a tyrannical sceptre.

Behold the enticing tune of remote work opportunities—a melodic rendition that elevates one's aspirations to work while wearing pyjamas and preparing meals at home. On the contrary, upon closer inspection, one realises that the remote work option is as readily available as an undisclosed garden concealed by IT security concerns and managerial scepticism.

Without overlooking the pièce de résistance—the annual holiday party—in the vast comedic opera of employee benefits, the document alludes to a jubilant spectacle, a carnival-style festivity. However, as reality unfolds, the budget for the celebration is comparable to that of a lemonade stand. The sole noteworthy aspect of the occasion is the boss's speech being inflated and the insatiable wealth of knowledge that you gain.

In broad strokes, esteemed colleagues, let us navigate the enigmatic realm of perks and quirks while maintaining a light-hearted demeanour and a chuckle deep within ourselves. Pupils and peculiarities within the domain of employee benefits perform a whimsical ballet, serving as a reminder that although the benefits document may make grandiose claims, our perspective is more likely to be confined to the confines of the office. Laughter abounds in the workplace, where the delightful quirks and irony of corporate perks serve as a satirical melody of the mundane and absurd.

Chapter 20:
Promotion and Politics

A promotion is much more than just a fancy new title; it is the evidence of your development, capacity for taking on greater responsibility, and dedication to exceeding your own limits. A trip into unfamiliar territory, where the top view offers more chances to make an impact on the business landscape and a new set of obstacles. These promotions are the sweet awards that all ambitious creatures in the corporate world long for. You, my dear colleagues, have embarked on an endeavour full of challenging tasks and calculated moves in an effort to reach the pinnacle. In order to get one, you must first demonstrate your skills like a business world Tarzan by swinging from vine to vine, dodging the occasional slingshot of office gossip, and navigating through the dense underbrush of office politics.

The person who rises to the top gets a bird's-eye view of the corporate wilderness below, in addition to reaping the rewards of achievement. You need a strong will and a decent sense of humour to make it through this crazy ride, my friend.

Additionally, there is a sacred ceremony known as "Promotion Politics" that must be observed in order to graduate. Hardworking employees shudder at the mere thought of it, and those who dare to dream of moving up the corporate ladder find their buried scepticism stirred. It's a game of calculated smiles, nuanced nods, and learning how to say a lot without really saying anything at all.

So here you are, walking that narrow tightrope of office gossip, trying not to trip over the banana peel, and traversing through the dense bushes, reaching for the roses of promotion. To navigate this precarious balance, it takes skill, precision, and a deftness of reading between the lines that would make Sherlock Holmes proud.

On the one hand, you're trying to make an impression, demonstrating your abilities, and praying that all of your hard work is appreciated. On the other hand, you're deciphering the unspoken rules of the office political chessboard, making moves that keep you in the game without getting entangled in the web of trickery.

To be worthy of this massive show, one must first prove it by showcasing an amazing capacity to take on more tasks, like an Atlas bearing the weight of the entire world on its shoulders. Forget about finishing your current tasks; the secret to success is to accumulate an ever-growing mountain of projects. This way, your workload will grow and accelerate daily, much like a snowball rolling down a hill.

Disguised as managers and supervisors, the corporate gods will be just as excited to hear about your acquired skills as a kid in a candy store. With glimmering eyes, they ask, "Can you juggle chainsaws while drafting an Excel spreadsheet?" "Oh, and don't forget to smile—we value positivity here."

The real challenge starts when you learn to multitask: getting noticed (achieving the much-discussed visibility in the eyes of grandmasters). The workplace becomes a theatrical production, with you, my dear employee, as the main attraction. You must perform every night, dancing down the aisles, to show your support for the cause. It's all about work-life spectacle these days; forget about work-life balance.

When the official day comes to an end at five o'clock, you will be taken to a parallel universe where overtime is the currency of success. Your star will shine brighter in the corporate constellation the longer you work. They say that sleep is for the weak, while you work through the night, sacrificing sleep for the sweet nectar of awareness.

But surprise! There's a plot twist coming! And just when you believe you've got the exposure and multitasking down pat, the promotion gods smile and tell you that someone else has outperformed you. It's an old story, a tragic comedy in which the main character dances nonstop, only to lose out to a dark horse who has a penchant for spreadsheet calculations on his fingertips, PowerPoint presentations, and, of course, the essential ability for water cooler and coffee break talks; who also knows the coffee flavour preferences and the correct timings.

Consequently, the vicious cycle continues, much like an endless round of musical chairs with never-ending music. Every worker has a turn, twirling and vaulting across obstacles to try and earn a promotion to the coveted top spot. Sadly, very few will rise above the others, leaving the others to ponder the absurdity of the corporate circus.

As this bittersweet saga comes to a close, remember, dear office warrior, that the path to success may not be juggling chainsaws or working long hours. Perhaps it's time to call the game's rules into question and rethink what it means to rise through the ranks in this quirky realm of Promotion Politics.

Heart is thriving for recognition!!

Flowing into the internal and external milieu,
Disguised in so many forms,
When the head is full,
Of exploration and conclusion,
And the heart is thriving for,
Recognition,
Personally and professionally,
In every permutation and combination,
Striving for perfection,
Discontentment stirs inside,
From unawareness and qualm,
And unable to stay calm,
For what we assume is mostly an illusion,
And the choices we're making all through,
Chasing the same old mental ruts,
For better or for worse,
In helter-skelter,
Of what might have been?
To what could be,
Are enough to be recognised,
Am I worth it?
The ceaseless chatter,
Rehashing the past,
Or rehearsing the future,
Full of fathomless thoughts,
Will I be recognised,

This season,
And valued for my contribution,
Or will they find,
A greater reason,
For a lil' less,
Drive and dedication,
OR will I receive,
A greater satisfaction,
Is bit by bit killing you!!

Reviews

"Mridula's versatility shines through in 'Tales from the Cubicles,' The book stands as a testament to Mridula's artistry, offering a rich tapestry of contemplation and discovery, while her dedication to corporate warriors adds a touch of inspiration and laughter to the corporate realm."

Gaurav Srivastava,
Director of Operations,
QBS Learning Inc.

The book "Tales from the Cubicles" provides a thoughtful exploration of the crucial role that corporate values play in the contemporary business landscape and how an employee needs to navigate through its madness. Written with a keen understanding of the evolving dynamics of the corporate world Mridula, the author, delves into the significance of fostering a values-driven culture.

One of the book's strengths lies in its ability to connect theoretical concepts with real-world examples. Through insightful case studies and anecdotes, the author illustrates how companies with a strong commitment to ethical values not only weather challenges more effectively but also build enduring relationships with stakeholders.

Rahul Borooah, GM Operations,
HarperCollins Publishers

"Tales from the Cubicles" brilliantly captures the essence of modern office life with humour and sharp insight. Mridula's vivid storytelling transforms everyday corporate scenes into a lively, contemporary adventure. It's a refreshing and relatable read for anyone navigating today's fast-paced professional world, blending satire with genuine wisdom. A true gem in the realm of modern workplace literature.

Saurabh Singh
Additional Commissioner of Income Tax

Tales from the Cubicles" is a like a beautiful Office Odyssey, written on account of characters, generally not counted in corporate lessons in high flying business journals. The whole narration is woven with wit, humour and human empathy about colourful creatures living vivid lives flourishing thousand feet deep below the wavy surface of corporate sea.

Shambhu Nath
Delivery Manager
TCS

Tales from the Cubicles thoroughly encapsulate the vibrant tapestry of modern corporate culture, intricately woven from the author's, deeply felt by her soul, and meticulously transcribed onto the pages. It's not just a narrative; it's a living, breathing reflection of the contemporary workplace, full of wit, humour, and satire- to make us laugh, shed a light on society and human behaviours; where the author Mridula's authenticity shines through every anecdote and observation.

> Wing Commander Vineet Gupta

Having spent over two decades in the corporate 'jungle', loved the hilarious take on everyday routines. You can't help but try to place names against each of the 'species'. A nice, light breezy read.

> Sudhir MS

An engaging read based on the author's varied experiences in the corporate world and skilfully transforming accepted aspects about it into humorous perspectives & stories!

> Rohit Vatsa
> IT Industry Veteran

Tales from the cubicle is a unique take on the corporate chronicles that most corporate employees will relish reading.

The author's keen observations and satirical take makes it a fun and relatable read. Must read!

> Abhishek
> Technical Project Manager
> Google LLC

If you are looking for a feel good, humorous and light hearted read, Tales from the cubicles is exactly what the doctor ordered. Every chapter effortlessly chronicles the daily grind of office in a subtle way that brings a chuckle to your face.

Reading this novel is like catching up with that one friend from office that forces you to appreciate the humour in fleeting everyday moments amidst the long and sometimes challenging workdays! At its heart this novel is charming and reminding us to embrace humour in everyday life! And that's an inspiring and lovely message.

Sudhir
GTM Strategy
Adobe

www.ingramcontent.com/pod-product-compliance
Lightning Source LLC
LaVergne TN
LVHW061617070526
838199LV00078B/7318